He did not ~~~~~~ ~~~~~~ ~~~~~~ ~~~~~~ **ers**
smoothed ~~~~~~ ~~~~~~ ~~~~~~ ~~~~~~
patterns fr~~~~~~ ~~~~~~ ~~~~~~ **avel,**
then back. ~~~~~~ ~~~~~~ **not unaffected**
by his touch, even now, Jessa blinked
down at him

He looked up then, and as their gazes met, Jessa
suddenly knew, with searing, gut-wrenching
certainty, exactly what he was doing.

Tariq was not touching her randomly. He was
not caressing her. He was tracing the faint
white lines that scored her belly—the stretch
marks she had tried to rub away with lotions
and creams, the lines more visible now in the
bright morning light than she remembered them
ever being before. They were the unmistakable
evidence that she had been pregnant.

The world stopped turning. Her heart stopped
beating. His eyes bored into her as his hands
tightened. He only waited.

And then, when he had stared at her so long she
was convinced he had ripped every last secret
from her very soul, his mouth twisted.

"I have only one question for you," he said,
every word like a knife. "Where is the child?"

All about the author...
Caitlin Crews

CAITLIN CREWS discovered her first romance novel at the age of twelve in a bargain bin at the local five-and-dime. It involved swashbuckling pirates, grand adventures, a heroine with rustling skirts and a mind of her own, and a seriously mouthwatering and masterful hero. The book (the title of which remains lost in the mists of time) made a serious impression. Caitlin was immediately smitten with romances and romance heroes, to the detriment of her middle-school social life. And so began her lifelong love affair with romance novels, many of which she insists on keeping near her at all times, thus creating a fire hazard of love wherever she lives.

Caitlin has made her home in places as far-flung as York, England, and Atlanta, Georgia. She was raised near New York City, and fell in love with London on her first visit when she was a teenager. She has backpacked in Zimbabwe, been on safari in Botswana and visited tiny villages in Namibia. She has, while visiting the place in question, declared her intention to live in Prague, Dublin, Paris, Athens, Nice, the Greek Islands, Rome, Venice and/or any of the Hawaiian islands. Writing about exotic places seems like the next best thing to moving to them.

She currently lives in California with her animator/comic-book-artist husband and their menagerie of ridiculous animals.

Caitlin Crews

MAJESTY, MISTRESS...
MISSING HEIR

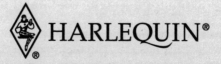

HARLEQUIN®

TORONTO • NEW YORK • LONDON
AMSTERDAM • PARIS • SYDNEY • HAMBURG
STOCKHOLM • ATHENS • TOKYO • MILAN • MADRID
PRAGUE • WARSAW • BUDAPEST • AUCKLAND

Recycling programs
for this product may
not exist in your area.

ISBN-13: 978-0-373-12950-8

MAJESTY, MISTRESS...MISSING HEIR

First North American Publication 2010.

Copyright © 2010 by Caitlin Crews.

www.eHarlequin.com

Printed in U.S.A.

MAJESTY, MISTRESS...
MISSING HEIR

CHAPTER ONE

JESSA glanced up from her desk automatically when the door to the letting agency was shoved open, and then froze solid in her chair.

It was like a dream—a dream she had had many times. He strode inside, the wet and the cold of the Yorkshire evening swirling around him like a great black cape.

She found herself on her feet without knowing she meant to move, her hands splayed out in front of her as if she could ward him off—keep him from stepping even further into the small office. Into her life, where she could not—would not—allow him to be, ever again.

"There you are," he said in a deep, commanding voice, as if he had satisfied himself simply by laying cold eyes upon her—as if, unaccountably, he had been looking for her.

Jessa's heart thudded against her ribs as her head spun. Was he an apparition, five years later? Was she dreaming?

"Tariq," she said, dazed, as if naming the dream could dispel it.

But Tariq bin Khaled Al-Nur did not look like a dream. He was nothing so insubstantial, or easily forgotten in the light of day. When she had known him he had claimed to be no more than a wealthy, overindulged member of his country's elite class; she knew that he was now its ruler. She hated that she knew—as if that knowledge was written across her face and might suggest to him that she had followed his every move across the years when the truth was, she had wanted only to forget him.

But she could not seem to pull her gaze from his.

Jessa found that all these years later she could remember every detail about Tariq with perfect, shocking clarity, even as the evidence before her made it clear that he was far better—far much *more*—than she had allowed herself to recall. His features were harder, more impenetrable. He was more of a *man,* somehow. It seemed impossible, but her memories had diminished him. The reality of Tariq was powerful, alive—dazzling.

Dangerous.

Jessa tried to concentrate on the danger. It didn't matter that her heart leaped when she saw him, even now. What mattered was the secret she knew she must keep from him. She had foolishly begun to hope that this particular day of reckoning would never come. She looked at him now, clear-eyed thanks to her shock, though that was not the improvement she might have hoped for.

He was hard-packed muscle in a deceptively lean form, all whipcord strength and leashed, impossible power beneath skin the color of nutmeg. Time seemed to stop as Jessa stood in place, cataloging the harsh lines of his face. They were more pronounced than she remembered—the dark slash of his brows beneath his thick black hair, the masculine jut of his nose, and the high cheekbones that announced his royal blood as surely as the supremely confident, regal way he held himself. How could she have overlooked these clues five years ago? How could she have believed him when he'd claimed to be no one of any particular importance?

Those deep green eyes of his, mysterious and nearly black in the early-evening light, connected hard with a part of her she thought she'd buried years before. The part that had believed every lie he'd told her. The part that had missed, somehow, that she was being toyed with by a master manipulator. The part that had loved him heedlessly, recklessly. The part that she feared always would, despite everything.

When he was near her, she forgot herself.

He closed the door behind him, the catch clicking softly on the doorjamb. It sounded to Jessa as loud as a gunshot, and she almost flinched away from it. She could not allow herself to be weak. Not with so much at stake! Because he must know what had happened. There could be no other reason for an appearance like this, here in the forgotten back streets of York at an office that was surely far beneath his imperial notice.

He must know.

With the door closed, the noise of the evening rush in York's pedestrian center disappeared, leaving them enclosed in a tense, uncomfortable silence. The office was too small, and felt tinier by the moment. Jessa's heart hammered against her chest. Panic dug sharp claws into her sides. Tariq seemed to loom over her, to surround her, simply by standing inside the door.

He did not move, nor speak again. He held her gaze with his, daring her to look away. Challenging her. He was effortlessly commanding even in silence. Arrogant. Fierce.

He was not the easygoing playboy she remembered. Gone was his quick smile, his lazy charm. This man was not to be trifled with. This man was the king who had always lurked within the Tariq she'd known, who she'd but glimpsed in passing here and there. A shiver traced cold fingers down her spine and uncurled in her belly.

He must know.

Her pulse sounded too loud in her ears. She could feel their tangled history and her secrets all around her, dragging at her, forcibly reminding her of the darkness she'd fought so hard to escape back then. But she had more to protect now than just herself. She had to think of Jeremy, and what was best for him. Wasn't that what she had always done, no matter the cost to herself?

She let her eyes travel over Tariq, reminding herself that he was just a man, no matter how fierce. And for all his regal bearing now, back then he had disappeared without so much as a word or a backward glance or a forwarding address. He was as treacherous and formidable as the exotic desert that was his home. The exquisitely tailored clothes he wore, silk and cashmere that clung to the bold, male lines of his body, did nothing to disguise the truth of him. He was a warrior. Untamed and wild, like a shock of brilliant color in the midst of grays and browns. He was a predator. She had known it then, on some deep, feminine level, though he had smiled and joked and concealed it. Her body knew it now, and horrified her by thrilling to it even as she fought for control. Her lungs felt tight, as if he sucked up all the air in the room.

She had never thought she would see him again.

She didn't know how to react now that he was in front of her.

"No," she said, astonished to hear that her voice sounded calm even when the world around her seemed to shimmer and shake. It gave her the courage to continue. It didn't matter how compelling he was. His being so compelling had been the problem in the first place! She squared her shoulders. "No. You cannot be here."

His dark brows rose, haughty and proud. His hair, thick

and black and a touch too long for civility, seemed to sparkle with the autumn rain from outside. He kept his impossible, haunting eyes trained on her face. How she had once loved those eyes, which had seemed so sad, so guarded. Tonight they seemed to see right through her. His expression was unreadable.

"And yet here I am." His voice was low, husky, and held the barest hint of the foreign lands he'd come from, wrapped in something both chocolate and smooth. *Dangerous.* And once more—a blatant, unmistakable challenge. It hit Jessa like a fist to the midsection.

"Without invitation," she pointed out, pleased her tone was just this side of curt. Anything to seem stronger than she felt. Anything to look tougher than she was. *Anything to protect Jeremy.*

"Do I require an invitation to enter a letting agent's?" he asked, unperturbed. "You must excuse me if I have forgotten British customs. I was under the impression places such as these encourage walk-in clientele."

"Do you have an appointment?" Jessa asked, forcing her jaw to stop clenching. It was what she would ask any other person who appeared off the street, wasn't it? And really, why should Tariq bin Khaled Al-Nur be any different?

"In a manner of speaking," he said, his tone hinting at some significance that was lost on Jessa, though she sensed he expected her to understand his meaning. "Yes."

His eyes traveled over her, no doubt comparing her to his memories. Jessa felt her cheeks flame, in some combination of distress and fury. She had the sudden worry that she fell short, and then could have kicked herself. Or, preferably, him. Why should she care about such things? Nothing would change the fact that she was an ordinary girl from Yorkshire and he was a king.

"It is nice to see you again, Jessa," Tariq said with a dangerous politeness that did not conceal the ruthlessness beneath. She wished he would not say her name. It was like a caress. It teased at the back of her neck, swirled through her blood, and traced phantom patterns across her skin.

"I'm afraid I can't say the same," she replied coolly. Because she had a spine. Because she needed to get rid of him, and make certain he never returned. Because their past was far too complicated to ever be brought out into the present. "You are the very last person I would ever wish to see again. If you go away quickly, we can pretend it never happened."

Tariq's dark jade eyes seemed to sharpen. He thrust his long, elegant hands into the pockets of his trousers with a casualness Jessa could not quite believe. The Tariq she'd known had been nonchalant, at ease, but that man had never existed, had he? And this man in front of her was nothing like the man Tariq had pretended to be. He was too hard, too fierce.

"I see the years have sharpened your tongue." He considered her. "What else has changed, I wonder?"

There was one specific way she had changed that she could not possibly share with him. Did he already know it? Was he baiting her?

"*I* have changed," Jessa said, glaring at him, deciding that an offense was better than any defense she might try to throw up against this strangely familiar man, who was much more like steel than the lover she remembered. "It's called growing up." She lifted her chin in defiance, and could feel her hands ball into fists at her sides. "I am no longer likely to beg for anyone's attention. Not anymore."

She did not see him move but she had the sense that he tensed, as if readying himself for battle. She braced herself, but he only watched her. Something too ruthless to be a smile curled in the corner of his hard mouth.

"I do not recall a single instance of you begging," Tariq replied, an edge in his dark voice. "Unless you mean in my bed." He let that hang there, as if daring her to remember. Mute, Jessa stared back at him. "But if you wish to reenact some such scene, by all means, do so."

"I think not," she gritted out from between her teeth. She would not think about his bed, or what she had done in it. *She would not.* "My days of clinging to pathetic international playboys are long past."

She felt the air tighten between them. His dark green eyes narrowed, and once again she was reminded that he was not a regular man. He was not even the man she had once known. He was too wild, too unmanageable, and she was a fool to underestimate him—or overestimate herself. Her weakness where he was concerned was legendary, and humiliating, and should have left her when he had.

But she could feel it—feel him—throughout her body, like nothing had changed, even though everything had. Like he still owned and controlled her as effortlessly and carelessly as he had years before. Her breasts felt tight against her blouse, her skin was flushed, and she felt a familiar, sweet, hot ache low in her belly. She bit her lip against the heat that threatened to spill over from behind her eyes and show him all the things she wanted to hide.

She knew she could not let this happen, whatever *this* was. She wanted nothing to do with him. There were secrets she would do anything in her power to keep from him. Chemistry was simply that: a chemical, physical reaction. It meant nothing.

But she did not look away.

* * *

She had haunted him, and Tariq bin Khaled Al-Nur was not a man who believed in ghosts.

He stared at the woman who had tortured him for years, no matter where he went or with whom, and who now had the audacity to challenge him with no thought for her own danger. Tariq considered himself a modern sheikh, a modern king, but he understood in this moment that if he had one of his horses at his disposal he would have no qualm whatsoever about tossing Jessa Heath across the saddle and carrying her away to a tent far off in the desert that comprised most of his homeland on the Arabian Peninsula.

In fact, he would enjoy it.

He was right to have come here. To have faced this woman, finally. Even as she called him names, and continued to defy him. Just as she had done so long before. His mouth twisted in a hard smile.

He knew that he should be furious that she wished to keep him at arm's length, that she dared to poke at him as if he was some insipid weakling. He knew that he should feel shame that he, Sheikh Tariq bin Khaled Al-Nur, King of Nur, had come crawling back to the only woman who had ever dared abandon him. The only woman he had ever missed. Who stood before him now in an ugly suit that did not become her or flatter her lushness, unwelcoming and cold instead of pleased to see him again. He should be enraged at the insult.

But instead, he wanted her.

It was that simple. That consuming. He had finally stopped fighting it.

One look at the curvy body he still reached for in his sleep, her wide eyes the color of cinnamon, her sinful, lickable mouth, and he was hard, ready—alive with need. He could taste her skin, feel the heat of her desire. Or he remembered it. Either way, he needed to be deep inside her once again.

Then, perhaps, they could see how defiant she really was.

"A pathetic playboy, am I?" he asked, keeping his tone light, though he could not disguise the intent beneath. This woman reminded him so strongly of his other, wasted life—yet he still wanted her. He would have her. "An intriguing accusation."

Temper rose in her cheeks, turning ivory to peach. "I can't imagine what that means," she snapped. "It is not an accusation, it's the truth. It is who you are."

Tariq watched her for a long moment. She had no idea how deep his shame for his profligate former existence ran within him. Nor how closely he associated her with all he had been forced to put behind him, and now found so disgusting. He had fought against her hold on him for years, told himself that he only remembered her because she had left him, that he would have left her himself if she'd given him the opportunity, as he had left countless other women in his time.

Still, here he was.

"It means that if I am a playboy, you by definition become one of my playthings, do you not?" he asked. He enjoyed the flash of temper he saw in her face much more than he should have. The warrior inside him was fully roused and ready to take on his opponent. "Does the description distress you?"

"I am not at all surprised to hear you call me a *plaything*." Her mouth twisted. "But I was never yours."

"A fact you made abundantly clear five years ago," he said drily, though he doubted she would mistake the edge beneath. Indeed, she stiffened. "But is this any way for old friends to greet each other after such a long time?" He crossed the room until only the flimsy barrier of her desk stood between them.

"Friends?" she echoed, shaking her head slightly. "Is that what we are?"

Only a few feet separated them, not even the length of his arm. She swallowed, nervously. Tariq smiled. It was as he remembered. She still looked the same—copper curls and cinnamon eyes, freckles across her nose and a wicked, suggestive mouth made entirely for sin. And she was still susceptible to him, even from across a desk. Would she still burn them both alive when he touched her? He couldn't wait to find out.

"What do you suggest?" she asked. Her delicate eyebrows arched up, and that sensual mouth firmed. "Shall we nip out for a coffee? Talk about old times? I think I'll pass."

"I am devastated," he said, watching her closely. "My former lovers are generally far more receptive."

She didn't like that. The flush in her cheeks deepened, and her cinnamon eyes darkened. She stood straighter.

"Why are you here, Tariq?" she asked, in a crisp, no-nonsense voice that both irritated and aroused him. She crossed her arms over her chest. "Are you looking to let a flat in the York area? If so, you'll want to return when the agents are in, so they might help you. I'm afraid they're both out with clients, and I'm only the office manager."

"Why do you think I'm here, Jessa?"

He studied her face, letting the question hang there between them. He wanted to see her reaction. To catalog it. Her fingers crept to her throat, as if she wanted to soothe the beat of her own pulse.

"I cannot imagine any reason at all for you to be here," she told him now, but her voice was high and reedy. She coughed to cover it, and then threw her shoulders back, as if she fancied herself a match for him. "You should go. Now."

And now she ordered him out? Like a servant? Tariq

shifted his weight, balancing on the balls of his feet as if readying himself for combat, and idly imagined how he would make her pay for that slight. He was a king. She should learn how to address him properly. Perhaps on her knees, with that sinfully decadent mouth of hers wrapped around him, hot and wet. It would make a good start.

"If you won't tell me what you want—" she began, frowning.

"You," he said. He smiled. "I want you."

CHAPTER TWO

"ME?" Jessa was taken aback. She would have stepped back, too, but she'd locked her knees into place and couldn't move. "You've come here for *me?*"

She did not believe him. She couldn't, not when his dark eyes still seemed laced with danger and that smile seemed to cut right through her. But there was a tiny, dismaying leap in the vicinity of her heart.

She could face the unwelcome possibility that she might still be a fool where this man was concerned, on a purely physical level. But she had absolutely no intention of giving in to it!

"Of course I am here for you," he said, his eyes hot. One black eyebrow arched. "Did you imagine I happened by a letting agent's in York by accident?"

"Five years ago you couldn't get away from me fast enough," Jessa pointed out. "Now, apparently, you have scoured the countryside to find me. You'll forgive me if I can't quite get my head around the dramatic change in your behavior."

"You must have me confused with someone else," Tariq said silkily. "You are the one who disappeared, Jessa. Not I."

Jessa blinked at him. For a moment she had no idea

what he was talking about, but then, of course, the past came rushing back. She had gone to the doctor's for a routine physical, only to discover that she had been pregnant. Pregnant! She had had no illusions that Tariq would have welcomed the news. She had known he would not. She had needed to get away from him for a few days to pull herself together, to think what she might do while not under the spell his presence seemed to cast around her.

Perhaps she hadn't phoned him. But she hadn't left him.

"What are you talking about?" she asked now. "I was not the one who fled the country!"

His mouth tightened. "You said you were going to the doctor, and then you disappeared. You were gone for days, and then, yes, I left the country. If that is what you want to call it."

"I came back," Jessa said, her voice a low throb, rich with a pain she would have said was long forgotten. "You didn't."

There was an odd, arrested silence.

"You will have heard of my uncle's passing, of course," Tariq said, his gaze hooded. His tone was light, conversational. At odds with the tension that held Jessa in a viselike grip.

"Yes," she said, struggling to match his tone. "It was in all the papers right after you left. It was such a terrible accident." She took care to keep her voice level. "Imagine my surprise when I discovered that the man I'd known as simply the son of a doctor was, as it happened, a member of the royal family and the new king of Nur."

"My father *was* a doctor." His brows rose. "Or do you think I impugned his honor after his death merely for my own amusement?"

"I think you deliberately misled me," she replied evenly, trying not to let her temper get the best of her. "Yes, your father was a doctor. But he was also the younger brother of a king!"

"You will forgive me," Tariq said with great hauteur, "if your feelings did not supercede legitimate safety concerns at the time."

How could he do that? How could he make her feel as if she had wronged him when *he* was the one who had lied and then abandoned her? What was the matter with her?

"Safety concerns?" she asked with a little laugh, as if none of this mattered to her. Because none of it *should* have mattered to her. She had come to terms with her relationship with Tariq years ago. "Is that what you call it? You invented a man who did not exist. Who never existed. And then you pretended to be that man."

He smiled. Jessa thought of wolves. And she was suddenly certain that she did not wish to hear whatever he might say next.

"I'm sorry about your uncle," she murmured instead, her voice soft. Softer than it should have been, when she wanted only to be strong.

"My uncle, his wife, and both of their sons were killed," Tariq said coolly, brushing off her words of condolence. The wolf smile was gone. "And so I am not just King of Nur now, but the very last of its ancient, founding bloodline. Do you know what that means?"

She was suddenly terrified that she knew exactly what that meant, and, more terrifying, what *he* would think it meant. She could not allow it.

"I imagine it means that you have great responsibilities," Jessa said. She couldn't think of any reason he would drop by her office in Yorkshire to discuss the line of succession in his far-off desert kingdom, save one. But surely, if he knew the truth, he would not be wasting his time here with her, would he? Perhaps he only suspected. Either way, she wanted him gone. "Though what would I know about it?" She spread her hands out, to encompass the letting office. "I am an office manager, not a king."

"Indeed." He watched her and yet he made no move. He only kept that dark green gaze trained upon her while the rest of his big, lean body seemed too still, too much raw power unnaturally leashed. As if he was poised and ready to pounce. "I am responsible to my people, to my country, in a way that I was not before. It means that I must think about the future." His voice, his expression, was mocking, but did he mock her, or him? "I must marry and produce heirs. The sooner the better."

All the breath left Jessa's body in a sudden rush. She felt light-headed. Surely he could not mean…? But there was a secret, hidden part of her that desperately hoped he did and yearned for him to say so—to make sense of these past lonely, bittersweet years by claiming her, finally, as his. To fulfill the foolish dream she'd always held close to her heart, and fervently denied. *His wife. Tariq's wife.*

"Don't be absurd," she chided him—and herself. She was nothing. A no one. He was the King of Nur. And even if he had been a regular, accessible man, he was also the only one with whom she had so much tangled history. It was impossible. It had always been impossible. "You cannot marry *me!*"

"First you mock me," Tariq said gently, almost conversationally. And yet the nape of Jessa's neck prickled in warning. "You call me a pathetic playboy. Then you order me to leave this place, like some insignificant insect, and now you scold me like a child." His lips curved into a smile that did not reach his eyes. "Perhaps you forget who I am."

She knew exactly who he was. She knew too well what

he could do to her. What he had done already. She was much more afraid of what he might do now.

"I have not forgotten anything, Tariq," she said, glad that her voice was calm yet strong, as it ought to be. Glad that she sounded capable and unmoved, as she should. "Which is why I must ask you to leave. Again."

Tariq shrugged with apparent ease, but his eyes were hot.

"In any case, you misunderstand me," he said. He smiled slightly. "I am not in the habit of proposing marriage to ex-lovers who harbor such disdain for me, I assure you."

It took a moment for his words to fully sink in. Humiliation followed quickly, thick and hot. It was a dizzying reminder of how she had felt when his mobile phone had come up disconnected, his London flat vacated, one after the other, with her none the wiser. Mortification clawed at her throat and cramped her stomach. Had she really imagined that he had appeared out of nowhere because he wished to *marry* her? She was unbearably foolish, again, as if the past five years had never happened.

But they had happened, she reminded herself. And she had been through far worse than a few moments of embarrassment. It was the memory of what she'd survived, and the hard choices she'd made, that had her pushing the humiliation aside and meeting his gaze. There were more important things in the world than Tariq bin Khaled Al-Nur, and her own mortification. Her cheeks might still be red, but her head was high.

"Then what is it you want?" she asked coolly. "I have no interest in playing games with you."

"I have already told you what I want," he said smoothly, but there was still that hard edge beneath. "Must I repeat myself? I do not recall you being so slow on the uptake, Jessa."

Once again, the way he said her name nearly made her shiver. She shook it off and tried to make sense of what he was saying but then, abruptly, gave up. Why was she allowing this to happen? He had waltzed in after all this time, and cornered her behind her desk? Who did he think he was?

With a burst of irritation, at herself and at him, Jessa propelled herself around the side of her desk and headed for the door of the office. She didn't have to stand there and let him talk to her this way. She didn't have to listen to him. He was the one who had had all the choices years ago, because she hadn't known any better and hadn't *wanted* to know any better, but she wasn't that besotted girl any longer. That girl had died years ago, thanks to him. He had no idea what she'd been through, and she didn't owe him anything, including explanations.

"Where do you imagine you can go?" he asked, in an idle, detached tone, as if he could not possibly have cared less. She knew better than to believe that, somehow. "That you believe I cannot follow?"

"I have some ideas about where you can go," Jessa began without turning back toward him, temper searing through her as she stalked toward the door.

But then he touched her, and she had not heard him move. No warning, no time to prepare—

He touched her, and her brain shorted out.

His long fingers wrapped around her arm just above the elbow. Even through the material of her suit jacket, Jessa could feel the heat emanating from him—fire and strength and his hard palm against her arm, like a brand. Like history repeating itself. Like a white-hot electricity that blazed through her and rendered her little more than ash and need.

He closed the distance between them, pulling her up hard against the unyielding expanse of his chest. She gasped, even as his other hand came around to her opposite hip, anchoring her against him, her back to his front, their two bodies coming together like missing puzzle pieces.

She could feel him everywhere. The sweet burn where his powerful body connected with hers, and even where he did not touch her at all. Her toes curled in her shoes. Her lungs ached. Deep in her belly she felt an intoxicating pulse, while between her legs she felt herself grow damp and ready. For him. All for him, as always.

How could her body betray her like this? How could it be so quick to forget?

"Take your hands off me," she demanded, her voice hoarse with an emotion she refused to name. At once, he stepped back, released her, and all that fire was gone. She told herself she did not feel a hollowness, did not feel bereft. She turned slowly to face him, as if she could not still feel the length of his chest pressed against her.

She thought of Jeremy. Of what she must hide.

Of what Tariq would do if he knew.

"Is this what you think of me?" she asked, her voice low, her temper a hot drumbeat inside her chest. She raised her chin. The hoarseness was gone as if it had never been. "You think you can simply turn up after all this time, after vanishing into thin air and leaving me with nothing but your lies, and I'll leap back into your arms?"

"Once again, you seem to be confused," Tariq said, his voice hushed, his gaze intent. Almost demanding. But there was something else there that made a shiver of silent warning slide along her spine. "I am not the one who ran away. I am the one who has reappeared, despite all the time that has passed."

"You are also the one who lied about who he was," Jessa pointed out. "Hardly the moral high ground."

"You have yet to mention where you disappeared to all those years ago," Tariq said, his voice sliding over her, through her, and making her body hum with an awareness she didn't want to accept. "Exactly what moral high ground are you claiming?"

And, of course, she could not tell him that she had found out she was pregnant. She could not tell him that she had suspected, even though she had loved him to distraction, that he would react badly. She could not tell him that after days of soul-searching, she had come back to London to share the news with him, only to find him gone as if he had never been. As if she had made him up.

And she certainly could not tell him that he was a father now. There was absolutely no doubt in her mind that Tariq's reaction to the news would be brutal. She sucked in a breath and forced a serene expression onto her face.

"The truth is, I have no interest in digging up the past," Jessa said. She shrugged. "I got over you a long time ago."

His eyes were like jade, and glittered with something darker.

"Is that so?" he asked in the same quiet voice, as if they were in the presence of something larger. She shoved the notion away, and had to restrain herself from reaching out and shoving *him* away, too. She knew better than to touch him.

"I'm sorry if you expected me to be sitting in an attic somewhere, weeping over your picture," Jessa said, trying to inject a little laughter into her voice, as if that might ease the tension in the room and in her own body. Tariq's eyes narrowed. "But I've moved on. I suggest you do the same. Aren't you a sheikh? Can't you snap your fingers and create a harem to amuse yourself?"

She thought for a tense, long moment that she had gone too far. He was, after all, a king now. And far more unnerving. But he looked away for a moment, and his mouth curved in something very nearly a smile.

"I must marry," Tariq said. Then he turned his head and captured her gaze with his. "But before I can do that particular duty, it seems I must deal with you."

"Deal with me?" She shook her head, not understanding. Not wanting to try to understand him. "Why should you wish to deal with me now, when you have had no interest in me for all these years?"

"You and I have unfinished business." It was a statement of fact. His eyebrows rose, daring her to disagree.

Jessa thought for a moment she might faint. But then something else kicked in, some deep protective streak that would not allow her to fall before this man so easily. He was formidable, yes. But she was stronger. She'd had to be.

Maybe, on some level, she had always known she would have to face him someday.

"We do not have unfinished business, or anything else," she declared, throwing down the gauntlet. She raised her chin and looked him in the eye. "Anything we had died five years ago, in London."

"That is a lie." His tone brooked no argument. He was the king, handing down his judgment. She ignored it.

"Let me tell you what happened to me after you left the country," Jessa continued in the same tone, daring him to interrupt her. His nostrils flared slightly, but he was silent. She took a step closer, no longer afraid of his nearness. "Did you ever think about it? Did it cross your mind at all?"

How proud she had been of that internship, straight out of university that long-ago summer. How certain she had been that she was taking the first, crucial steps to a glittering, high-powered career in the city. Instead, she had met

Tariq in her first, breathless week in London, and her dreams had been forever altered.

"You were the one who left—" he began, frowning.

"I left for two and half days," she said, cutting him off. "It's not quite on a par with what you did, is it? It wasn't enough that you left the country, disconnected your mobile phone, and put your flat up for sale," she continued, keeping her gaze steady on his. "Actually telling me you no longer wished to see me was beneath you, I suppose. But you also withdrew your investments."

His frown deepened, and his body tensed. Did he expect a blow? When he had been the one to deliver all of them five years ago, and with such cold-blooded, ruthless efficiency? Jessa almost laughed.

"What did you think would happen?" she asked him, an old anger she had thought she'd forgotten coloring her voice. She searched the dark green eyes she had once artlessly compared to primeval forests, and saw no poetry there any longer. Only his carelessness. "I was the intern who was foolish enough to have an affair with one of the firm's biggest clients. I had no idea you were *the* biggest client. And it was smiled upon as long as I kept you happy, of course."

Jessa could picture the buttoned-up, hypocritical investment bankers she had worked for back then. She could see once more the knowing way they had looked at her when they thought she was just one more fringe benefit the firm could provide for Tariq's pleasure. Just another perk. A bottle of the finest champagne, the witless intern, whatever he liked. But then he had severed his relationships—not only with Jessa, but with the firm that handled his speculative investments, all in the span of three quick days following the September Bank Holiday.

"I thought it best to make a clean break," he said, and there was strain in his voice, as if he fought against some strong emotion, but Jessa knew from experience that his emotions were anything but strong, no matter how they might appear.

"Yes, well, you succeeded in breaking something," she told him, the anger gone as quickly as it had come, leaving only a certain sadness for the girl she had been. "My career. Into tiny little pieces. They sacked me, of course. And once they did, who do you think wanted to hire the promiscuous intern who'd lost her previous firm so much money along with such a high-profile client?"

His mouth flattened and his eyes flashed that dark jade fire. But Jessa remembered the look of disgust on the senior partner's face when he'd called her into his office. She remembered the harsh words he'd used to describe her behavior, the same behavior that had received no more than a wink and a smile the week before. She'd stood there, pale and trembling, unable to process what was happening. She was pregnant. And Tariq had not only left her so brutally, he had left England altogether, to become a king. On top of all that, he had never been the person he'd claimed to be, the person she'd loved. It was all a lie.

"And that was the end of my brilliant career in London," Jessa said in a quiet, matter-of-fact manner. She tilted her head slightly to one side as she considered him. "I suppose I should thank you. It takes some people a lifetime to figure out that they're not cut out for that world. Thanks to you, it took me only a few short months."

"My uncle was killed," Tariq said in a low, furious voice, his body seeming to expand as he stood in the middle of the office floor, taking over the entire space. "I was suddenly thrust upon the throne, and I had to secure my position. I did not have time to soothe hurt feelings half the world away."

"They don't have notepaper or pens where you come from, then," Jessa said sarcastically, pretending she was unaffected by his magnetism, his power. "Much less telephones. Perhaps you communicate using nothing save the force of your royal will?"

He looked away then, muttering something harsh in a language she was just as happy she didn't know. In profile, he was all hard edges except for his surprisingly mobile mouth. He looked like the king he was. Noble features, royal bones. The sort of profile that would end up stamped on coins.

When she thought about it that way, the absurdity of the situation was almost too much for her. They should never have met in the first place—it was all too fantastical. It was one thing to dream of fairy-tale princes when one was fresh out of university and still under the impression that the world was waiting only to be bent to one's will. Tariq bin Khaled Al-Nur had always been too sophisticated, too dangerous, *too much* for the likes of Jessa Heath, and that was long before he became a king. She was a simple person, with a simple life and, once, a few big dreams, but she'd quickly learned the folly of dreams. She knew better now.

"Never fear," she said, folding her arms over her chest. "I'm a survivor. I picked myself up, dusted myself off, and made myself a life. It might not be the life I wanted when I was twenty-two, but it's mine." She lifted her chin and fixed her eyes on him, unafraid. "And I like it."

There was another silence. A muscle worked in Tariq's jaw, though he was otherwise motionless. Jessa had said things she had once only dreamed about saying, and that had to count for something, didn't it?

"There is no apology I can make that will suffice," Tariq said then, lifting his head to catch her gaze, startling her with his seeming sincerity. "I was thoughtless. Callous."

For a moment Jessa stared back at him, while something seemed to ease inside of her. Almost as if it was enough, somehow, that he had heard her. That he offered no excuses for what he had done. And perhaps it might have been enough, if that had been the end of what his abandonment had cost her. But it had only been the beginning. It had been the easy part, in retrospect.

"Congratulations," she said sarcastically, thinking of everything she'd suffered. The impossible decision she'd made. The daily pain of living with that decision ever since, no matter how much she might know that it was the right one. "You have managed to avoid apologizing with such elegance, I nearly thanked you for it."

"It is obvious that I owe you a great debt," he said then. If she hadn't been staring straight at him, she might have missed the flash of temper that came and went in his eyes. And she couldn't shake the strange notion that he meant to say something else entirely.

"There is no debt," she told him, stiffening. If he owed her something, that meant he might stay in the area, and she couldn't have that! He had to go, back to his own world, where he belonged. Far away from hers.

"I cannot make up for the loss of your prospects," Tariq continued as if she hadn't spoken. His voice was both formal and seductive. An odd mix, yet something inside her melted. "And perhaps there is nothing you wish for that I can provide."

"I've just told you I don't want anything," she said, more forcefully. "Not from you."

"Not even dinner?" He didn't quite smile. He inclined

his head toward her. "It is getting late. And I have wronged you. I think perhaps there is more to it, and the very least I can do is listen to you."

She didn't trust him for a second, much less his sudden gallantry and concern. She knew exactly how manipulative he could be. He'd lied to her for months and she'd bought it, hook, line, and sinker! And she had not forgotten that he'd said they had unfinished business between them. She should refuse him outright, demand he leave her alone.

But she didn't do it.

She was still buzzing from the unexpected rush she'd gotten when she'd told him exactly what he'd done to her. When she'd laid it out, piece by piece, and he'd had no defense. She had no intention of sharing the rest of it with him, but she'd be lying if she didn't admit that she liked being the one in charge. Perhaps she wasn't quite ready to dismiss him. Not quite yet. Was it that she felt powerful, or was it that melting within?

It was by far the most terrifying moment of the day.

"I'm afraid that's impossible," she told him stiffly, appalled at what she had nearly done. Was she mad? "I already have plans."

"Of course." Something passed through his eyes and made her catch her breath. "I understand. Another time, perhaps."

"Perhaps." She was noncommittal. Surely there could be no other time? Surely he would simply vanish back into the ether as he had before?

"Until then," he murmured, and then he turned and let himself back out of the office door. Jessa had the sense of his body moving like liquid into the night, and then she was alone.

He was gone as abruptly as he had come.

Jessa let out a breath, and sagged where she stood,

finding herself on her knees in the center of the industrial blue carpet. She pressed her hands against her face, then let them drop.

The room was again just a room. Just an office. Without Tariq crowding into it, it was not even small.

Jessa stayed where she was until her breathing returned to normal. She had to think. She was not foolish enough to believe that he was gone for good, that he might have hunted her down in York for a simple conversation most regular people would have on the telephone, or via the Internet, or not at all. The crazy part of her that still yearned for him swelled in the knowledge that he would, inevitably, return, and she felt something like a sob catch in her throat. She had come to terms with having loved and lost Tariq years ago. She had had no other option. But she had never expected that he would swing back into her life like this. She had never dreamed she would see him again, unless it was on the television.

She excused herself for being so uncharacteristically overwhelmed. He was an overwhelming man, to say the least! Jessa climbed to her feet and smoothed her hands over her skirt, straightening her ill-fitting suit jacket with a quick tug. If only she could set her world to rights as easily. It was one thing to mourn the man she had loved so much she'd let him change the course of her whole life while she was on her own these past years. It was something else again when he was in front of her. But she couldn't allow any of that to distract her from the main point.

Because all that mattered now was Jeremy.

The child she had fiercely and devotedly cared for while she'd carried him inside of her for nine long months. The baby she had kissed and adored when he'd finally decided to greet the world after so many hard, lonely hours of painful labor, his face red and his tiny fists waving furiously in front of him.

The son she had loved so desperately that she'd given him up for adoption when he had been four months old despite how agonizing that decision had been—and how hard it continued to be—for her. The son she still loved enough to fight with everything she had to maintain his privacy, his happiness, no matter the cost.

No matter what she might have to do.

CHAPTER THREE

JESSA was not surprised to find Tariq at her front door the following morning. If anything, she was surprised he had waited the whole of the night before reappearing. It might have lured her into a false sense of security had she not known better.

Perhaps she did still know him after all.

She opened the door to his peremptory knock because she knew that simply ignoring him would not only fail to deter him, it might also rouse her neighbors' interest and Jessa didn't want that. She didn't want someone noticing that the King of Nur was lounging about outside her otherwise unremarkable terraced house on a quiet Fulford side street just outside York's medieval walls. What good could come of drawing attention to the fact they knew each other? She needed to get him to go back to his own country, his own world, as quickly as possible.

She cracked the door as little as she could, and stood in the wedge, as if she was capable of keeping him out with her body if he wanted to come in.

Their eyes caught and held. Time seemed to halt in its tracks. Jessa felt her heart quicken its pace to thud heavily against her ribs, and her breath caught in her throat.

She was aware on some level that the morning was gray and wet, but the weather faded from her notice, because *he* was all she could see. And he was distressingly, inarguably real. Not the figment of her imagination she had half convinced herself he had been, conjured from the depths of her memory to torture herself with the night before. Not a dream, not even a nightmare.

"Good morning, Jessa," he said, as casually as if he spent all of his Saturday mornings fetched up on her doorstep, looking impossibly handsome and as inaccessible as ever.

He was no hallucination. He was flesh, blood, and all male, packed into one deceptively lean and powerful body. Today he wore black jeans and a tight black jersey that hugged the muscular planes of his chest and announced that whatever else the King of Nur might do while enjoying his luxurious lifestyle, he kept himself in top physical condition. His jade eyes burned into hers, nearly black in the morning gloom.

"I didn't make you up, then," Jessa said in as even a tone as she could manage. She wanted to order him to leave her alone, but she suspected he would pounce on that and use it against her, somehow. Best not to hand the warrior any weapons. "You're really here."

"How could I stay away?" he asked, with one of those predatory smiles that managed to distract her even as it unnerved her. She did not believe that he was here simply for her, no matter what he claimed. What was the likelihood that the lover who had had no qualm discarding her so completely would have a sudden drastic change of heart five years later, apropos of nothing? *Slim,* she had decided sometime in the early morning hours, long after she'd given up on sleeping. *Slim to none and bordering on less than zero.*

He had to know about Jeremy. Didn't he?

"You do not believe me," he murmured. He leaned in closer, taking up far too much space, blocking out the world behind him. "Perhaps I can convince you."

The good part about this situation, Jessa thought as he moved closer, close enough that she could smell the familiar, haunting scent of sandalwood and spice and his own warm skin, was that it made her choices very simple. There was only one: ease his fears and suspicions however she could, and send him on his way.

She told herself she could do this. Her head felt too light, her knees too weak. But she would do what she must, for her son's sake. She could handle Tariq. She could. She stepped back and opened the door wider.

"You'd better come in."

Tariq let Jessa lead him inside the house, which felt dark and close as all English dwellings felt to him. This whole country of low clouds and relentless rain made him crave the impossibly blue skies of Nur, the horizon stretching beyond imagining, the desert wide and open and bright. The fact that he was not where he was supposed to be, where he needed to be—that he was still in England when he should be at the palace in Azhar handling the latest threat of a rebel uprising near the disputed border— reminded him too much of his playboy past. Yet he had still come to find her.

He had no time for this. He had no patience for ghosts or trips through the past. It was finished. He was no longer that self-indulgent, wasteful creature, and had no wish to revisit him now. Yet she had haunted him across the years, as no other woman ever had. He could recall her smile, the arch of her back, the scent of her skin, in perfect detail. He had

had no choice but to find her. He had to exorcize her once and for all, so he might finally get on with his life as he should have done five years ago. Marriage, heirs. His duty.

Jessa walked before him into her sitting room, and came to a stop beside the mantel. Slowly, she turned to face him, her tension evident in the way she held herself, the way she swallowed nervously and pulled at her clothes with her hands. He liked that she was not at ease. It made his own uncertainty less jarring, somehow. She could deny it all she liked, but he could feel the awareness swell between them.

Tariq's eyes swept the room, looking for clues about this simple woman who made him feel such complicated things, so complicated he had tracked her down after all this time, like a besotted fool. The sitting room was furnished simply, with an eye toward comfort rather than glamour. The sofa seemed well used and neat rather than stylish. A half-drunk cup of tea sat on the coffee table, with the remnants of what he assumed to be toast. There were a few photographs in frames beside her on the mantelpiece—a family of three with a mother he took to be Jessa's sister. Others of the sisters together, as small children, then with Jessa as a gawky teenager.

Her eyes were wide and cautious, and she watched him apprehensively as he finally turned his attention to her. If she thought to hide her responses from him, it was much too late. He was as attuned to her body as to his own.

Tariq reminded himself that he could not simply order her to his bed, though that would be far simpler than this dance. He did not know why she resisted him. But he was not an untried boy. He could play any games she needed to play. He picked up the nearest photograph and frowned down at it.

"You resemble your sister," he said, without meaning to comment. "Though you are far more beautiful."

Jessa's cheeks colored, and not with pleasure. She reached over and jerked the photograph from his hand, leaving him with only a blurred impression of her less attractive sister, a fair-haired husband, and their infant held between them.

"I won't ask what you think you're doing here," she said in a low, controlled voice. But he could see the spark of interest in her eyes.

"By all means, ask." He dared her, arching his brows and leaning closer, crowding her. He liked the lick of fire that scraped across his skin when he was near her. He wanted more. "I am more than happy to explain it to you. I can even demonstrate, if you prefer." She did not step away, though her color deepened.

"I don't want to know how you justify your behavior," she retorted. She tilted her chin into the air. "We have nothing to discuss."

"You could have told me this on the doorstep," he pointed out softly. "Why did you invite me into your home if we have nothing to discuss?"

She looked incredulous. "Had I refused to answer the door, or to let you in, what would you have done?"

Tariq only smiled. Did she realize she'd conceded a weakness?

"This game will not last long if you already know I will win it," he said. His smile deepened. "Or perhaps you do not wish for it to last very long?"

"The only person playing a game here is you," Jessa retorted.

She put the photograph back on the mantel and then crossed her arms over her chest as she faced him. He moved closer. He stretched one arm out along the mantel and shifted so that they were nearly pressed together, held back only by this breath, or the next. She stood her ground, though he could see it cost her in the pink of her cheeks, hear it in the rasp of her breath. He was close enough to touch her, but he refrained. Barely. He could see her pulse hammer against the side of her neck. It was almost unfair, he thought with a primal surge of very male satisfaction, that he could use her body against her in this way. Almost.

"You keep testing me, Jessa," he whispered. "What if I am no match for it? Who knows what might happen if I lose control?"

"Very funny," she threw back at him, her spine straight though Tariq could tell she wanted to bolt. Instead, she scoffed at him. "When is the last time that happened? Has it *ever* happened?"

Unbidden, memories teased at him, of Jessa sprawled across the bed in his long-ago Mayfair flat, her naked limbs flushed and abandoned beneath him. He remembered the rich, sweet scent of her perfume, her unrestrained smile. The low roll of her delighted laughter, the kind that started in her belly and radiated outward, encompassing them both. The lush swell of her breasts in his hands, her woman's heat against his tongue. And the near-violent need in him for her, like claws in his gut, that nothing could satiate.

He didn't understand all the ways he wanted her. He only knew that she had burrowed into him, and he had never been able to escape her, waking or sleeping. She was his own personal ghost. She haunted him even now, standing so close to him and yet still so far away.

He looked away from her for a moment, fighting for control. She took that as a response.

"Exactly," she said as if she'd uncovered a salient truth. "You are not capable of losing control. No doubt, that serves you well as a king."

Tariq turned his head and found her watching him, color high on her cheeks and her cinnamon-brown eyes bright. Did she mean to insult him? Tariq did not know. But he did know that he was more than a match for her. There was one arena where he held all the power, and both of them knew it.

"You misunderstand me," he murmured. He reached over and slid his hand around the back of her neck, cupping the delicate flesh against his hard palm and feeling the weight of her thick, copper curls. She jumped, then struggled to conceal it, but it was too late. He could feel her pulse wild and insistent against his fingers, and he could see the way her mouth fell open, as if she was dazed.

He did not doubt that she did not *want* to want him. He had not forgotten the days she had disappeared, which had been shockingly unusual for a girl who had always before been at his beck and call, just as he had not forgotten his own panicked response to her unexpected unavailability, something he might have investigated further had history and tragedy not intervened. But there was no point digging into such murky waters, especially when he did not know what he would find there. What mattered was that she still wanted him. He could feel it with his hands, see it in the flush of her skin and the heat in her gaze.

"Tariq—" she began.

"Please," he murmured, astounded to hear his own voice. Astonished that he, Sheikh Tariq bin Khaled Al-Nur, would beg. For anything, or any reason. And yet he continued. "I just want to talk."

Was he so toothless, neutered and tame? But he could not seem to stop himself. He had to see this through, and then, finally, be rid of her once and for all. If there was another way, he would have tried it already. He *had* tried it already!

"About us."

* * *

Us. He'd actually said the word *us.*

The word ricocheted through Jessa's mind, leaving marks, much like she suspected his hand might do if he didn't take it off her—if she didn't burst into flame and burn alive from the slight contact.

As if there had ever been an *us* in the first place!

"You have to get on with your life," her sister Sharon had told her, not unkindly, about two weeks after everything had come to such a messy, horrible end in London and Jessa had retreated to York. Crawled back, more like, still holding the secret of her pregnancy close to her chest, unable to voice the terrifying truth to anyone, even her sister. And all while Tariq's face was on every television set as the tragedy in Nur unfolded before the world. The sisters had sat together in Jessa's small bedroom while Sharon delivered her version of comfort. It was brisk and unsentimental, as Sharon had always been herself.

"I don't know what that means," Jessa had said from the narrow bed that had been hers as a girl, when Sharon had taken the reins after their parents died within eighteen months of each other. Eight years older, Sharon and her husband Barry had taken over the house and, to some extent, the parenting of Jessa, while they tried and failed to start their own family.

"It means you need to get your head out of the clouds," Sharon had said matter-of-factly. "You've had an adventure, Jessa, and that's more than some people ever get. But you can't lie about wallowing in the past forever."

Tariq hadn't felt like the *past* to Jessa. Or even an *adventure.* Even after everything that had happened—after losing her job, her *career*, her self-respect; after finding herself pregnant and her lover an unreachable liar, however little she might have come to terms with that—she still yearned for him. He'd felt like a heart that beat with hers, louder and more vibrant inside her chest than her own, and the thought of the gray, barren life she was expected to live without him was almost more than she could bear. She had choked back a sob.

"Men like him are fantasies," Sharon had said, with no little pity. "They're not meant for the likes of you or me. Did you imagine he'd sweep you off to his castle and make you his queen? You, little Jessa Heath of Fulford? You always did fancy yourself something special. But you've had your bit of fun and now it's time to be realistic, isn't it?"

Jessa had had no choice but to be realistic, she thought now. But Tariq was back and there was far too much at stake, and she still couldn't think straight while he touched her. And he wanted to talk about *us*, of all things.

"There is no *us*," she said crisply, as if she was not melting, as if she was still in control. She met his gaze squarely. "I'm not sure there ever was. I've no idea what game you thought you were playing."

"I have a proposition for you," he said calmly, as if what she'd said was of no matter. He lounged back against the mantelpiece, letting his hand move from her skin slowly. He was every inch the indolent monarch.

"It is barely half-nine and here you are propositioning me," Jessa replied, determined to get her balance back. She kept her voice dry, amused. Sophisticated, the way she imagined the glamorous women he was used to would speak to him when he propositioned them. "Why am I not surprised?"

If her heart beat faster and her skin felt overheated, and

she could still feel his hand on her like a tattoo, she ignored it.

"Am I so predictable?" His hard face looked cast in iron in the low gloom from the front windows. And yet Jessa sensed that the real shadows came from within him.

She stood ramrod straight because she could not allow herself to move, to back away from him. She thought it would show too much, be too much of a concession. She laced her fingers together in front of her as tightly as possible.

"It is not a question of whether or not you are—or were—predictable," she said coolly. She raised her eyebrows in unmistakable challenge. "Perhaps you were simply like any other man when things got too serious. Afraid."

He stilled. The temperature in the room seemed to plunge. Jessa's heart stuttered to a halt. She knew, suddenly, that she was in greater danger from him in that moment than ever before. Something dark moved across his face, and then he bared his teeth in something far too wild to be a smile.

"Proceed with care, Jessa," he advised her in a soft voice that sent a chill snaking down her spine. "Not many people would dare call a king a coward to his face."

"I am merely calling a spade a spade," Jessa replied, as if she did not have a knot of trepidation in her stomach, as if she was not aware that she was throwing pebbles at a lion. She shook the loose tendrils of her hair back from her face, wishing her curls did not take every opportunity to defy her. "You were not yet a king when you ran away, were you?"

"Ran away?" he echoed, enunciating each word as if he could not quite comprehend her meaning.

"What would you call it?" she asked coolly. Calmly. She even smiled, as if they shared a joke. "Adults typically have conversations with each other when an affair is ending, don't they? It's called common courtesy, at the very least."

"Again," he said, too quietly, "you have forgotten the sequence of events. You were the one who disappeared into thin air." He stood so still, yet reminded Jessa not of a statue, but of a coiled snake ready to strike. Yet she couldn't seem to back down.

"I merely failed to answer my mobile for two days," Jessa replied lightly. "That's not quite the same thing as quitting the country altogether, is it?"

"It is not as if I was on holiday, sunning myself on the Amalfi Coast!" Tariq retorted.

Jessa shook her head at him. "It hardly matters now," she said carelessly, as if her heart hadn't been broken once upon a time. "I'm only suggesting that perhaps it was a convenient excuse, that's all. An easy way out."

Tariq was so still it was as if he'd turned to stone. He studied her as if he had never seen her before. She had the sudden, uncomfortable notion that he was assessing her as he might an enemy combatant on the field of battle, and was coldly scanning her for her weaknesses. Her soft points.

And all the while that awareness swirled around them, making everything seem sharper, brighter.

"I will not explode into some dramatic temper tantrum, if that is your goal with these attacks," Tariq said finally, never looking away from her. She felt her cheeks heat, whether in relief or some stronger emotion, she didn't know. "I will not rage and carry on, though you question my honor and insult my character." His hard mouth hinted at a curve, flirted with it. "There are better ways to make my feelings known."

She refused to feel the heat that washed through her. She would not accept it. The tightness in her belly was agitation, worry, nothing more. But the desperate, purely feminine part of her that still wanted him, that thirsted for his touch in ways she could not allow herself to picture, knew better.

"What, then?" she demanded, unable to pull her gaze from his. What was this intoxicating fire that burned between them, making her ask questions she knew she did not want the answers to? "What is your damned proposition?"

"One night." He said it so easily, yet with that unmistakably sensual edge underneath.

Somewhere deep inside, she shuddered, and the banked fire she wanted to deny existed flared into a blaze.

His gaze seemed to see into her, to burn through her.

"That is all, Jessa. That is what I want from you."

CHAPTER FOUR

TARIQ'S words echoed in the space between them, bald and naked and challenging. Jessa swallowed. He saw her hands tremble, and a kind of triumph moved through him. She could not control what would happen. Perhaps she even knew it. But she did not back down. She still thought she could fight him. It made him want her all the more.

He knew, even if she did not, that she was going to end this confrontation in his bed. Beneath him, astride him, on her knees before him—he didn't care. He only knew that he would win, and not only because he always won. But because he would accept no other outcome, not with this woman. Not when she had been in his head for all these years.

Because he already knew how this would end, he could be patient. He could wait. He could even let her fight him, if she wished it. What would it matter? It would only make it that much better in the end.

"I don't want to misunderstand you again," she said after a long moment. She searched his face, her own carefully blank.

He realized that he liked this grown-up, self-assured version of Jessa. He liked that she stood up to him, that she was mysterious, that she was neither easily read nor easily intimidated. When was the last time anyone had defied him?

"One night of what?" she asked.

"Of whatever I want," he said softly, pouring seduction into every syllable. "Whatever I ask."

"Be specific, Tariq," she said, an edge to her voice. He interpreted it as desire she would have preferred not to feel.

"As you wish," he murmured. He leaned toward her, pleased with the way she jerked back, startled, and the way her breath came too quickly. "I want you in my bed. Or on the floor. Or up against the wall. Or all of the above. Is that specific enough?"

"No!" She threw one hand into the air as if to hold him back, but it was too late for that. Tariq moved closer and leaned toward her, until her outstretched palm pressed up against his chest. Her hand was the only point of contact between them, her fingers trembling in the hollow between the hard planes of his pectoral muscles.

She did not drop her hand. He did not lean back.

"No, what?" he asked with soft, sensual menace. "No, you do not wish to give me that night? Or no, you do not want to hear how I will sink inside you, making you clench and moan and—"

"Don't be ridiculous!" She whispered the words, but her eyes glazed with heat and something else, and the hand she held between them had softened into a caress, touching him rather than holding him off.

"It is many things," Tariq said in a low voice, "but it is not ridiculous."

He took her hand in his and, never looking away from her, raised her wrist to his lips. He tasted her, her skin like the finest silk, and her pulse beneath it, fluttering out her excitement, her distress. It was like wine and it went to his head, knocking into him with dizzying force.

She made some sound, as if she meant to speak. Perhaps she did, and he could not hear her over the roaring in his ears, his blood, his sudden hardness. He had not expected the surge of lust so sharp and consuming. It barreled through his body from their single point of contact, making him burn. Making him *want*.

It was worse now that he touched her, now that he was before her, than it had been when he only remembered. Much worse.

"I want you out of my system," he told her, his voice urgent and deep. Commanding, because he meant it more than he had just moments before. Because he was desperate. He needed a queen and he needed heirs, and she was what kept him from doing that duty. He had to erase the hold she had on him! "Once and for all. I want one night."

One night.

Jessa stared at Tariq in shock for a moment, as the impossible words shimmered between them like heat. The breathtaking strength of his hard chest against her palm made her whole arm ache, and the ache radiated through her, kicking up brushfires everywhere it touched. Her mind could not seem to process what he'd said, but her body had no such difficulty. She felt her breasts swell in reaction, her nipples hardening into tight, nearly painful points that she was grateful he couldn't possibly see beneath the wool sweater she'd thrown on earlier. Between her legs, she ached, even as her body readied itself for him. Awareness, thick and heavy and intoxicating, thrummed through her. She was electric.

And he was watching her.

Jessa could no longer bear his proximity. And why was she still touching him? Why had she let the moment draw out? No longer caring that he might see it as a victory—only needing space between them—she snatched her hand away from the heat of his body and moved to the other side of the room. There was only her coffee table between them when she stopped, but it was something. It made her feel slightly less hysterical, slightly less likely to pretend the past five years had never happened and fling herself into his arms. How had she lost control of herself so quickly?

"I beg your pardon," she began in her stiffest, most formal tone.

"Do you?" he interrupted her, leaning so nonchalantly against her mantel, so big and dark and terrifying, with all of that disconcerting, green-eyed attention focused intently upon her. He was like her own personal fallen angel, come to take her even further into the abyss. She had to remember why she could not let him. "Do not beg my pardon when there are so many more interesting things you could beg me for."

He was so seductive even when she knew better. Or perhaps it was only that she was so susceptible and weak where he was concerned. She could feel his hands on her, though he had not moved. Her palm itched with the need to soothe itself against the steellike muscles of his chest once more. How could her body want him, still? She had been so sure she was over him, finally. She had been certain of it. She had even, recently, begun to imagine a future in which Tariq was not the shadow over her life, but a bittersweet memory.

"You must be joking," she said, because that was what she might say if her body wasn't staging a full-scale revolt—if, in fact, she felt as she ought to feel toward this man. It had taken her five years to get over him once. What would it be like a second time? It didn't bear considering.

"I assure you, I have no sense of humor at all where you are concerned," he said.

Somehow, she believed him. And yet there was a certain gleam in his dark eyes that convinced her she was better off not knowing exactly what he meant by that remark.

"Then you are insane," she declared. "I would no more spend one night with you then I would prance naked down Parliament Street!"

As she heard it echo around her lounge, it occurred to her that a wise woman might not have used the word *naked* in front of this man, in defiance of this man. Tariq did not seem to move, and yet at the same time he seemed to grow larger. Taller, darker, *more*. As if he blocked all the exits and kept her chained where she stood, all because he willed it. How did he do such a thing? Had he always been so effortlessly irresistible? In her memories, he had taken over every room he had ever entered with the sheer force of his magnetism, but she had supposed that to be her own infatuation at play, not anything he did himself.

"What I mean," she said when he simply studied her in that hawkish, blood-stirring way that made her mouth go dry and made her wonder if she might be more his prey than she knew, than she wanted to know. "What I mean is that of course I will not spend a night with you. There is far too much water under the bridge. I'm surprised you would ask."

"Are you?" He looked supremely unconcerned. Imperial. A brow arched. "I did not ask."

Of course he had not actually asked. Because he was the King of Nur. He did not need to ask. He needed only to incline his head and whatever he desired was flung at his feet, begging for the chance to serve him. Hadn't she done the same five years ago?

He had no more than glanced at her across the busy office that fateful day and Jessa had been his. Just like that. It had been that immediate and all-consuming. She had not even waited for him to approach her. As if she was a moth drawn inexplicably and inexorably to the flame that would be the death of her, she had risen to her feet and then walked toward him without so much as a thought, without even excusing herself from the conversation she was taking part in. She had no memory of moving, or choosing to go to him. He had merely looked at her with his dark sorcerer's eyes and she had all but thrown herself at him.

And that had been while he was playing his game of pretending to be a doctor's son with some family money, but otherwise of interest to no one. Now he was no longer hiding—now he was a king. No wonder he seemed so much more powerful, so much more alluring, so much more devastating.

"Then you have saved me the trouble of refusing you," Jessa said, fighting to keep her voice calm, with all the tension ratcheting through her. "Good thing you did not bother to ask."

"Why do you refuse?" Tariq asked quietly, straightening from the mantel. It was as if he stepped directly into her personal space, crowding her, though he was still all the way across the room. Jessa eased away from him, from the powerful energy he seemed to exude like some kind of force field, but she had to stop when the backs of her knees hit the couch.

You cannot run, she warned herself. *He would only chase you. And you must think of Jeremy. You must!*

"Why do you want one night?" Jessa retorted. She

shoved her hands into the pockets of her trousers, trying to look calm even if she didn't feel it. "And why now? Five years is a bit too long for me to believe you've been carrying a torch." She laughed at the very idea, the sound dying off when he only looked at her, a truth shimmering in his dark gaze that she refused to accept.

"I told you that I must marry." He shrugged, as if a lifelong commitment was no more interesting to him than a speck of dust. Perhaps it was not. "But first I wanted to make sure you were no longer a factor. You can understand this, can't you?"

"I would have thought I ceased being any kind of factor some time ago," Jessa said. Was her tone the dry, sophisticated sort of tone she'd aimed for? She feared it was rather more bitter than that, and bit her lower lip slightly, wishing she could take it back.

Tariq rubbed at his chin with one hand, still watching her closely, intently, as if he could see directly into her.

"Who can say why certain things haunt a man?" He dropped his eyes. "After my uncle died, my life was no longer my own. My every breath and every thought was of necessity about my country. It was not enough simply to accept the crown. I had to learn how to wear it." He shook his head slightly, as if he had not meant to say something so revealing. He frowned. "But as it became clear that I could not delay my own marriage further, I knew I could not marry with this history hanging over me. And so I resolved to find you. It is not a complicated story."

This time, when he looked at her, his dark green eyes were even more unreadable than before.

"You expect me to believe that you..." She couldn't bring herself to say it, it was too absurd. "There is no history hanging over us!"

"You are the only woman who has ever left me," he told her. His tone was soft, but there was a hard, watchful gleam in his gaze. "You left an impression."

"I did not leave you!" she gritted out. There was no way to explain why she had gone incommunicado for those days—she who had rarely been out of his sight for the wild, desperate weeks of their affair.

"So you say." He shrugged, but his attention never left her face. "Call it what you wish. You were the only one to do it."

"And this has led you to track me down all these years later," Jessa said softly. She shook her head. "I cannot quite believe it."

The air around them changed. Tightened.

"Can you not?" he asked, and there was something new in his voice—something she could not recognize though she knew in a sudden panic that she should. That her failure to recognize it was a serious misstep.

Satisfaction, she thought with abrupt insight, but it was too late.

He crossed the room, rounded the coffee table in a single step and pulled her into his arms.

"Tariq—" she began, panicked, but she had no idea what she meant to say. All she could feel were his arms like steel bands around her, his chest like a wall of fire against hers. And all she could see was his hard face, lit with an emotion she could not name, serious as he looked down at her for a long, breathless moment.

"Believe this," he said, and fitted his mouth to hers.

CHAPTER FIVE

JESSA'S world spun, until she no longer knew if she stood or if she fell, and the mad thing was that she didn't much care either way.

Not as she wanted to. Not as she should.

Tariq's hard, hot mouth moved on hers and she forgot everything. She forgot all the reasons she should not touch him or go near him at all. She forgot why she needed to get rid of him as quickly as possible, so that he could never find out her secrets. So that he could not hurt her again as easily as he'd done before.

None of that seemed to matter any longer. All she cared about was his mouth. All she wanted was *more*.

He knew exactly how to kiss her, how best to make her head spin in dizzy circles. Long, drugging strokes as he tasted her, sampling her mouth with his, angling his head for a better, sweeter fit.

"Yes," she murmured, barely recognizing her own voice.

Sensation chased sensation, almost too much to bear. His strong hands moved over her, one flexed into the thick mass of her hair at the nape of her neck while the other splayed across the small of her back, pressing her hips against his. His clever, arousing mouth moved slick and hot against hers. Fire. Heat. Awe. The potent mix of vibrant memory and new, stunning sensation. Touching him was the same, and yet so very different. He tasted like some heady mix of spices, strong and not quite sweet, and she was drunk on it, on him, in seconds.

She could feel him everywhere, pumping through her veins, wrapped around each beat of her heart as it pounded a hectic rhythm against her chest. How had she lived without this for so long? She could not get close enough to him. She could not breathe without breathing him in. She could not stop touching him.

She let her hands explore him, trailing down the length of his impossibly carved torso, like something sculpted in marble, though his skin seemed to blaze with heat beneath her hands. He was nothing as cold as stone. He was so big, bigger than she remembered, and huskier. His strong shoulders were far wider than his narrow hips, his muscles hard from some kind of daily use. She traced patterns across the breadth of his lean back, feeling his strength and his power in her palms.

Tariq muttered something she could not understand. His hands stroked down the length of her back to cup her bottom, urging her closer until she was pressed tight against his thighs and the rock-hard maleness between them. She gasped. She felt her core melt and tremble against him. He sighed slightly, as if in relief. Jessa heard a distant crooning sound and realized, only dimly, that it came from her.

And still, he kissed her. Again and again. As if he could not stop. As if he, too, remembered that it had always been this way between them—this dizzying, terrifying rush of lust and need and *now*. Jessa could not seem to shake the memories that scrolled through her mind, each more sensual than the last, or the shocking fact that this was real, that they were doing this, all these years later.

She could not think. She could not imagine why she *should* think.

She twined her arms around his neck, arching her back to press her swollen, tender breasts against the hard planes of his chest, tilting her head back to give him better access. He did not disappoint. He broke from her mouth, his breathing harsh, and kissed his way down her cheek, her neck. His mouth was like a hot brand against her skin.

"More," he whispered, and his hands went to the hem of her sweater, pulling it up past her hips, then pausing when he uncovered her breasts. He looked at them for a long moment, as if drinking them in. Then he caressed each puckered nipple and tight globe in turn, shaping them through the camisole she wore, while Jessa moaned in mindless, helpless pleasure. Her sex ached, and she could feel an answering heat behind her eyes. She felt burned alive, eaten whole. She wanted more than his hands. She *wanted*.

Muttering a curse, Tariq stripped the sweater from her body, guiding her head through the opening with his strong, sure hands. He tossed it aside without glancing at it, and then paused for a moment to look down at her, his hard eyes gleaming in the gray morning light. The expression she read there made her belly clench, and pulse to a low, wild drum within.

Jessa's nipples stood at attention, tight and begging for his mouth. She could feel the hungry, restless heat in her core, begging for his mouth, his hand, his sex. Even her mouth was open slightly and softened, swollen from his kisses, begging for more of the same.

Could actual begging be far behind? How soon before she was right where she swore she'd never be again—literally on her knees, perhaps? Clutching desperately at him as he walked away once more?

The thought was like cold water. A slap. Jessa blinked, and sanity returned with an unwelcome thump, jarring her.

She staggered backward, away from him, out of reach of his dangerous hands. How could she have let this happen? How could she have allowed him to touch her like this?

Again, she thought wildly. *How can he do this* again?

"Stop," she managed to say, pushing the word out through the hectic frenzy that still seized her. He had broken her heart five years ago. What would he do this time? What else could he break? It had taken all these years to come to a place of peace about everything that happened, and here she was, tumbling right back into his arms again, just like before.

She hadn't believed that he could want her then, and she didn't believe it now, not deep inside of herself. She had never known what game he had been playing and what had led a man like him to notice someone like her. And here she was, much older and wiser, about to make the same mistake all over again! Just like last time, he would leave her when he was finished with her. And he *would* finish with her, of that she had no doubt. The only question was how much of herself she would turn over to him in the meantime, and how far she would have to go to get herself back when he left her, shattered once more.

No. She could not do this again. She would not.

"You do not want to stop," he said in that dark, rich voice that sent her nerve endings into a joyful dance and made her that much more resolute. "You only think that you do. Why think?"

"Why, indeed?" she asked ruefully, trying to pull herself together. She stood up straight, and smoothed her palms over the mess of her hair. She was afraid to look into the mirror on the far wall. She felt certain she didn't wish to know how she looked just now. Wanton and on the brink of disaster, no doubt.

"Whatever else passed between us, there is still this," Tariq continued, just short of adamant. "How can we ignore it?"

His voice tugged at her, as if it was something more than sex for him. As if it could ever be anything more than that, with this man! Why hadn't she learned her lesson?

"I won't deny that I'm still attracted to you," Jessa said carefully, determined that her inner turmoil should not come out in her voice. That she should somehow transmit a calmness she did not feel. "But we are adults, Tariq. We are not required to act on every last feeling."

"We are not *required* to, no," Tariq replied smoothly, a perfect echo of the easy, tempting lover he had been before, always willing to pursue passion above all else. It was how he had lived his life. He even smiled now, as if he was still that man. "But perhaps we should."

Jessa took a moment to reach over and draw her sweater toward her, trying to take deep, calming breaths. She pulled it back over her head as if it were armor and might protect her. She smoothed the scratchy wool material down over her hips, and then adjusted the heavy copper spill of her hair, pushing it back over her shoulders. Then she realized she was fidgeting. He would read far too much into it, and so she stilled herself.

How could she want him, as if it were no more than a chemical decision, outside of her control? Yes, of course, he was a devastatingly handsome man. There was no denying it. If he were a stranger and she saw him on the street, Jessa would no doubt find him enthralling. Captivating. But he was not a stranger. He was Tariq bin

Khaled Al-Nur. She knew him too well, and she had every reason in the world to be effectively allergic to him. Instead, she melted all over him and had to bite the inside of her cheek to keep from asking for more.

Begging for more, even.

She wanted to be furious with herself. But what she was, instead, was terrified. Of her own responses, her own reaction to him. Not even of Tariq himself.

"I thought perhaps you wished to talk about something of import," she said, sounding merely prim to her own ears, when she wanted to sound tough. She cleared her throat and then indicated the two of them with her hand. "*This* is not something I want. It's not something I need in my life, do you understand?"

"Is your life so full, then?" His dark eyes bored into her. His mouth was serious, flat and firm. "You never think of the past?"

"My life is full enough that the past has no place." She raised her chin, a bolt of pride streaking through her as she thought about how she had changed since he had known her. In ways both seen and unseen, but she knew the difference. She wondered if he could see those differences, but then told herself it hardly mattered. "It would not seem so to a king, I imagine, but I am proud of my life. It's simple and it's mine. I built it from scratch, literally."

"And you think I cannot understand this? That I cannot grasp what it is to build a life from nothing?" He shifted his weight, reminding Jessa that they were standing far too close to the sofa, and that it would be much too easy to simply fall backward and take him with her, letting him crush her so deliciously against the sofa cushions with his—

Enough! she ordered herself. *You cannot allow yourself to get carried away with him!*

"I know you cannot possibly understand," she replied. She moved then, rounding the coffee table and putting more space between them. She had always thought her sitting room was reasonably sized, a bit roomy, even. Now it felt like the inside of a closet. Or a small box. She felt there was nowhere she could go that he could not reach her, should he wish to. She felt trapped, hemmed in. *Hunted.* So why did something in her rejoice in it? "Just as I do not pretend to understand the daily life of the ruler of a country. How could I? It is beyond imagination."

"Tell me, then," he said, tracking her as she moved toward the window, then changed direction. "Tell me what it is like to be Jessa Heath."

"How could I possibly interest you?" she demanded, stopping in her tracks. She threw him an incredulous look. "Why would you want to know anything so mundane?"

"You would be surprised at the things I want to know." He slid his hands into the pockets of his dark jeans and considered her for a moment. Once more, Jessa was certain there was more going on than met the eye. As if, beneath those smooth words he hid sharp edges that she could only sense but not quite hear. "I have told you that you have haunted me across the years, yet you do not believe it. Perhaps if you told me more about yourself, I would find you less fascinating."

"I am a simple woman, with a simple life," she told him, her voice crackling with a kick of temper that she did not entirely understand. She didn't believe that he was mocking her. But neither did she believe that she could have fascinated him. With what? Her utter spinelessness? Or had he truly believed that she had left him and was one of those men who only wanted what he thought out of reach?

"If you are as proud of this life as you claim, why should

you conceal it?" he asked, too reasonably. Too seductively. "Why not seek to sing it from the rooftops instead?"

Frustrated, Jessa looked away for a moment, and felt goose bumps rise along her arms. She crossed them in front of her and tried to rub at her shoulders surreptitiously. She just wanted him to leave. Surely once he did, everything would settle back into place, as if he had never been.

"I would think you as likely to be interested in watching paint dry as in the life and times of an ordinary Yorkshire woman," she said in a low voice.

"It is possible, I think, that you do not know me as well as you believe you do," Tariq said in a haughty, aristocratic voice. No doubt he used this exact tone when ordering his subjects about. No doubt they all genuflected at the sound of it. But Jessa was not one of his subjects.

"My life is not a great story," she threw at him, daring him to judge her and find her lacking, yet knowing he could not fail to do so. "I wake up in the morning and I go to work. I like my job and I'm good at it. My boss is kind. I have friends, neighbors. I like where I live. I am happy." She could feel the heat in her eyes, and hoped he would think it was nothing more than vehemence. She wished she could convince herself of it. "What did you expect? That my life would be nothing but torment and disaster without you?"

His mouth moved, though he did not speak. It was tempting to tell him exactly how much she had suffered, and why—but she knew better. If he did not know too much already, then he could not know about Jeremy, ever. What was done was done. Tariq might think she did not know him, but she knew enough to be certain that he would handle that news in only one, disastrous way. And if he was only going to disappear again—and she knew without a single doubt that he was—she knew she couldn't risk telling him about Jeremy.

"Please go," she said quietly. She couldn't look at him. "I don't know why you came to find me, Tariq, but it's enough now. We did not require a reunion. You must leave."

"I leave tonight," he said after a moment, and her gaze snapped to his, startled. "You seem skeptical," he taunted her softly. "I am devastated that you find me so untrustworthy. Or is it that you did not expect me to go?"

"I hope you found what you were looking for here," she said, unable to process the various emotions that buffeted her. Intense, all-encompassing relief. Suspicion. And a pang of something she refused to call loss. "It was not necessary to dredge up ancient history, however."

"I am not so sure I agree," Tariq mused. His mouth looked so hard and incapable of the drugging kisses she knew he could wield with it. "Have dinner with me, tonight." He paused. Then, as an afterthought, as if he was unused to the word, he added, "Please."

Jessa realized she was holding her breath, and let it out.

"I don't think that's a good idea," she said, frowning, but more at herself than at him. Why did something in her want to have dinner with him—to prolong the agony? What could she possibly have to gain? Especially when there was so much to lose—namely, her head and her heart?

"If it is a good idea or a bad one, what does it matter?" Tariq shrugged. "I have told you I am leaving. One dinner, that is all. Is that too much to ask? For old time's sake?"

Jessa knew she should refuse him, but then what would he do? Show up here again when she least expected it? Somehow, the idea of him in her house at night seemed far more dangerous—and look what had happened already in broad daylight! She could not let him come back here. And if that meant one more uncomfortable interaction, maybe it was worth it. She was a grown woman who had told herself for years now that she had been an infatuated child when she'd met Tariq, and that the agony of losing him had been amplified by the baby she had carried. It had never occurred to her that seeing him again might stir up such strong feelings. It had never crossed her mind that she could still harbor any feelings for him! Maybe it was all for the best that she finally faced them.

And anyway, it was in public. How dangerous could even Tariq be in a roomful of other people?

In the back of her mind, something whispered a warning, but it was too late. Her mouth was already open.

"Fine," she said. It was for the right reasons, she told herself. It would bring closure, no more and no less than that. "I will have dinner with you, but that is all. Only dinner."

But she was not certain she believed herself. Maybe she could not be trusted any more than he could.

Satisfaction flashed across his face, and his mouth curved slightly.

Jessa knew she'd made a terrible mistake.

"Excellent." He inclined his head slightly. "I will send a car for you at six o'clock."

CHAPTER SIX

IT WAS only when Jessa found herself seated at a romantic table out on the fifth-story terrace of one of the finest houses she had ever seen, improbably located though it was in Paris, France, not far from the Arc de Triomphe, that she accepted the truth she had known on some level from the moment she'd so thoughtlessly agreed to this dinner: she was outmatched.

"I am pleased you could make it," Tariq said, watching her closely for her reaction. Jessa ordered herself not to give him one, but she could feel her mouth flatten. Had he had any doubt she would come?

"I was hardly given any choice, was I?" she asked. He had played her like the proverbial fiddle, and here she was, out of the country and entirely within his power.

Tariq only smiled arrogantly and waved at the hovering servant to pour the wine.

They sat outside on the terrace that circled the top floor of the elegant home, surrounded by carved stone statuary and wrought iron, the Paris night alive around them with lights and sounds. Yet Jessa could not take in the stunning view laid out before her, much less the beautiful table set with fine linen and heavy silver. Her head still whirled until she feared she might faint. She stared at Tariq from her place across from him while conflicting emotions crashed through her, but he only smiled slightly indulgently and toyed with the delicate crystal stem of his wineglass. And why should he do anything else?

She had taken care to wear her best dress, there was no pretending otherwise. If it was within the realm of possibility for someone like her to impress him, she'd wanted to do it—and now the royal-blue sheath dress she'd felt so pretty in earlier felt like sackcloth and ash against her skin, outclassed as it was by the splendor of Paris and what she knew was simply *one* of the homes Tariq must own.

How had she ever dreamed she could compete with this man, much less fascinate him in any way, no matter what lies he told? And the most important question was *why* had she wanted to do so in the first place? What did she hope to win here? She knew that he desired her, but she had already learned exactly how much stock he put in such things, hadn't she? As her sister had told her years before, *at the end of the day you're not the type a man like that will marry, are you?*

Whatever happened tonight, Jessa could never tell herself she hadn't known better.

Of her own free will she had stepped into the car he'd sent. She hadn't complained when, instead of delivering her to some appropriately luxurious hotel in the York area that might live up to the expectations of a king, whatever those might be, it had taken her instead to the Leeds Bradford Airport. She hadn't uttered a sound when she was handed aboard the impressive private jet by his ever-courteous, ever-solicitous staff. She'd told herself some story about Tariq's self-importance and had imagined she would make cutting remarks to him about his having to fly down to London for dinner. She had even practiced the sort of urbane, witty things she might say as she relaxed against the deep, plush leather seats and accepted a glass of wine from the friendly and smiling air hostess.

But then one hour had turned to two, and she had found herself emerging not in London at all, but in Paris. France.

To whom, exactly, should she complain? Tariq hadn't even been aboard the plane to compel her to come here. The scary thing was that Jessa knew full well that she had compelled herself.

"You cannot be angry with me," Tariq said softly, his voice low but no less intense. Jessa could feel the rich, slightly exotic sound of it roll through her, as if he'd hit some kind of tuning fork and her body was springing to attention. He nodded toward the view of stately buildings and glittering monuments in the cool night air, then returned his dark gaze to hers. "Such beauty forbids it."

"Can I not?" Jessa folded her hands in her lap and resolved to keep the hysteria at bay no matter what else happened. And if she was honest, what she felt when she looked at him was not hysteria, or anger. It was far more complicated than that.

"You agreed to dinner," Tariq said with a supremely arrogant shrug. A smile played with the corner of his mouth but did not quite take root there. "You did not specify where."

"Silly me," Jessa said. She met his eyes calmly, though it cost her something. "It never occurred to me that one was required to designate a preferred country when one agreed to a meal." *Under duress,* she wanted to say but did not. It wasn't entirely true, was it?

"There are many things that have not occurred to you, it seems," Tariq replied. Jessa did not care to explore the layers or possible meanings in that remark.

"You mean because of your vast wealth and resources," she said instead, as if she was used to discussing such things with various members of assorted royal families. "It is only to be expected when one is a king, isn't it? Surely these things would be much more impressive if they were the result of your own hard work and sweat."

"Perhaps," he said, a dark, affronted edge in his voice, though he did not alter his position. He continued to lounge in his chair like the pasha she supposed he really was. Only his gaze sharpened, piercing her, reminding her that she insulted him at her peril—and only because he allowed it.

"Do you find royalty offensive, Jessa?" he asked in a drawl. His brows rose, mocking her. "You English have a monarch of your own, I believe."

"The Queen has yet to whisk me off to a foreign country for a dinner that would have been uncomfortable enough in the local chip shop," Jessa retorted.

"It will only be uncomfortable if you wish it so," Tariq replied with infuriating patience, as if he knew something she did not. This time he really did smile, and it was not reassuring. "I am perfectly at ease."

"Somehow, that is not soothing," Jessa said, with the closest thing to a real laugh that she had uttered yet in his presence. It surprised them both. He looked startled as their eyes met and held. The moment seemed to stretch out and hover, locking Jessa in the green depths of his eyes with the glorious shine and sparkle of Paris stretching out behind him.

Her gaze drifted to his mouth, that hard, almost cruel mouth that could smile so breathtakingly and could do things to her that made her feel feverish to imagine. She felt her own lips part on a breath, or perhaps it was a sigh, and the world seemed to narrow and brighten all at the same time. She felt the now familiar coiling of tension in her belly, and the corresponding melting in her core. She felt the arch of her back and the matching curve of her toes inside her shoes. She began to *feel* each breath she took, as her heart kicked into a heavy, drugging rhythm that reminded her too well of his mouth upon her own, his hands on her skin.

Suddenly, brutally, the veil lifted. And Jessa realized in a sudden jolt, with an almost nauseating mixture of self-awareness and deep, feminine certainty, that this was exactly why she had come so docilely, so easily. Across borders, onto private planes, with nary a whisper of protest. This was why she had taken such pains in her bath earlier, dabbed scent behind her ears and between her breasts. She had told herself she was putting together her feminine armor. She had told herself she would dress the same way for any person she wished to appear strong in front of, that it was not romantic in the least to want to look her best or pin her hair up into a French twist or wear her most flattering and most lethal shoes. She had lied to herself, even as something within her knew the truth and had cried out for the wicked royal-blue dress that exposed her shoulders, kissed her curves and whispered erotically over her legs.

She had come here for him. For Tariq. For this raging passion that coursed through her veins and intoxicated her, this all-consuming desire that the intervening years and her own sacrifices had failed to douse in any way.

With a muttered oath that even she wasn't sure was a cry of desperation or a simple curse, Jessa rocked forward and to her feet. Restlessly—agitation making her body feel jerky and clumsy—she pushed herself away from the table and blindly headed toward the wrought-iron railing that seemed to frame the Paris street five stories below her feet as much as protect her from falling into it.

The truth seemed as cold as the autumn night, now that she had moved away from the brazier that hovered near the table—and the far more consuming fire that Tariq seemed to light in her.

She wanted him. Arguing with herself did nothing to stop it. She had spent the whole day determined to simply not be at home when he sent his car for her, and yet she had found herself immersed in the bath by half past four. She had ordered herself not to answer the door when the driver rang, but she had had the door open and her wrap around her shoulders before he could press the button a second time.

"Surely this should not distress you," Tariq said from behind her. Too close behind her, and once more she had not heard him move. Jessa closed her eyes. If she pretended, it was almost as if he was the magical, trustworthy lover she had believed him to be so long ago, and she the same starry-eyed, besotted girl. "It is a simple dinner, in a lovely place. What is there to upset you here?"

What, indeed? Only her own betrayal of all she'd thought she believed, all she thought she had gained in the years since his departure. What was that next to a luxurious meal on a Paris rooftop with the man she should avoid above all others?

"Perhaps you do not know me as well as you think," she replied, her voice ragged with all the emotion she fought to keep hidden. Or perhaps she did not know herself.

"Not for lack of trying," Tariq murmured. "But you will keep your mysteries, won't you?"

It was no surprise when his warm, strong hands cupped her shoulders, then stretched wide to test her flesh against his fingers, sending inevitable currents of desire tingling down her arms. She let out a sigh and bowed her head.

Perhaps this was inevitable. Perhaps this had always been meant to happen, somehow. She had never had the chance to say her goodbyes to Tariq, her fantasy lover, had she? She had run away to a friend's flat in Brighton to get her head together. The man she had loved had disappeared, and she learned soon after that he had never existed. But there had been no warning, no opportunity to express her feelings with the knowledge that it was their last time together.

A rebellious, outrageous thought wormed its way through her then, making her catch her breath.

What if she took, instead of lost? What if she claimed, instead of letting herself be deprived? What if she was the one in control, and no longer so passive, so submissive? What if she was the one who needed to get him out of her system, and not the other way around?

She turned in his loose grip, and leaned against the railing, tipping her head back so she could look him in the eye. What if she made this about what *she* wanted?

And what she wanted was the one last night she'd never had. She wanted to say her goodbyes—and it didn't hurt that in giving him one night, in taking it for herself, she was acknowledging that it could never be more than that between them. This was a memory, nothing more.

"I will give you one night," she said, before she lost her nerve. And then it was said, and there was no taking it back.

He froze. His face lost all expression, though his dark eyes glittered with jade fire. She had surprised him. *Good.*

"I beg your pardon?" he asked, enunciating each word very carefully, as if he thought he had misheard her, somehow. It made Jessa feel bolder. "What do you mean?"

"Must I repeat myself?" she asked, taking too much pleasure in tossing his own words back at him. She felt the power of this choice surge through her. She was the one in charge. She was the one who decided whether or not she would burn on this particular fire. And then she would walk away and finally be done with him. It would be like being reborn. "I don't recall you being so slow—"

"You must forgive me," he interrupted her with precious little civility, his teeth bared in something not at all as mild as a smile. "But why would you change your mind so suddenly?"

"Maybe I've considered things in a different light," Jessa said. Did she have to explain this to him, when she could hardly explain it to herself? She raised her brows. "Maybe I'm interested in the same things that you're interested in. Putting the past behind us, once and for all."

"For old time's sake?" he asked. He moved closer, his big body seeming to block out the City of Lights. Tension radiated from every part of him, and she knew she should be afraid of what he could do to her, what he could make her feel. She knew she should feel intimidated, outmatched once again.

But this was the one place where it didn't matter if he was a king and she a commoner. He wanted her with the same unwelcome intensity that she wanted him. In this, at least, they were equals. They matched.

She felt her mouth curve slightly into a smile that was as old as time, and spoke of a knowledge she had never put into words before, never felt so completely, down into her bones.

"What do you care?" she taunted him softly, daring him, challenging him.

His eyes went darker, his mouth almost grim with the passion she could feel surging through her veins.

"You are right," he said, his voice hoarse, and rough against her, though she welcomed it. Exulted in it. "I do not care at all."

His mouth came down on hers in something like fury, though it was much sweeter. Once again, he tasted her and went wild, and yet he merely kissed her, angling his head to better plumb the depths of her mouth, to intoxicate himself with her, with the feel of her soft body pressed against his. Her softness to his hardness. Her moan against his lips.

He had been prepared to seduce her if he had to. He had not been prepared for her to be the aggressor, and the surprise of it had desire raging through him.

"Be certain this is what you want," he growled, lifting his head and scanning her expression with fierce intensity. Her eyes were glazed with passion, her lips swollen from his kisses. Surely this would put an end to all the madness, all the nights he'd woken and reached for the phantom woman who was never there.

"Have I asked you to stop?" she asked, her breath uneven, her tone pure bravado. She tilted her stubborn chin into the air. "If you've changed your mind—"

"I am not the one who required so many games to achieve this goal," he reminded her, passion making his voice harsh. "I made my proposal from the start, hiding nothing."

"It is up to you," she said, her eyes narrowing in a maddening, challenging manner, her words infused with a certain strength he didn't understand. Who did Jessa Heath think she was that she so consistently, so foolishly, stood up to him, all the while refusing to tell him anything about her life, claiming she could only bore him? He could not recall the last person who had defied, much less taunted, him. Only Jessa dared.

A warning bell rang somewhere deep inside of him, but he ignored it.

"You will find that most things are, in fact, up to me," he replied, reminding them both that he, not she, was the one in charge, no matter how conciliatory he might act when it suited him.

He was a king. He might not have been born to the position, and he might have spent the better part of his life as an embarrassment to the man who had been, but he'd spent the past five years of his life atoning. He was in every way the monarch his uncle would have wished him to be, the nephew he should have been while his uncle lived. No imprudent and foolish woman could change that, not even this one, whom he realized he regarded as a kind of specter from his wastrel past. He would never fully put that past behind him until he put her there, too.

Jessa reached out her hand and placed it against his cheek. Tariq's mind went suddenly, scorchingly, blank as electricity surged between them.

"We can talk, if that is what you want," she said, as calmly as if discussing the evening's dinner menu. As unaffected, though he could feel the slight tremor in her delicate palm that belied her tone. "But it is not what I want."

"And what is it you want?"

"I do not want to talk," she said distinctly, purposefully, holding his gaze, her own rich with suggestion and the desire he was certain was written all over him. "And I don't think you want to, either. Do you?"

"Ah, Jessa," he said on a sigh, while a kind of moody triumph pumped through him and pulsed hard and long into his sex. She thought she was a match for him, did she? She would learn. And soon enough he would have her exactly where he wanted her. "You should not challenge me."

She cocked her head to one side, not cowed in the least, with the light of battle in her cinnamon eyes, and smiled.

It went directly to his head, his groin. He reached for her without thought, without anything at all but need, and pulled her into his arms.

CHAPTER SEVEN

IT WAS not enough. Her taste, her scent, her mouth beneath his and her hands tracing beguiling patterns down his chest. He wanted more.

"I want to taste you," he whispered in Arabic, and she shuddered as if she could understand him.

He wanted everything. Her surrender. Her artless, unstudied passion. The past back where it belonged, and left there.

But most of all, he wanted her naked.

Tariq raked his fingers into her hair, never lifting his mouth from hers, sending her hairpins flying and clattering against the heavy stones at their feet. Her heavy mass of copper curls tumbled from the sophisticated twist at the back of her head and fell in a jasmine-scented curtain around her, wild and untamed, just as he wanted her. Just as he would have her.

He lifted his mouth from hers and took a moment to study her face. Why should he spend even an hour obsessing over this woman? She was no great beauty, like some of the women he had been linked with in the past. Her face would never grace the covers of magazines nor appear on twelve-foot-high cinema screens. Yet even so, he found he could not look away. The spray of freckles across her nose, the sooty lashes that framed her spice-colored eyes—combined with her courtesan's mouth, she was something more unsettling than beautiful. She was… viral. She got into the blood and stayed there, changing and growing, and could not be cured using any of the usual methods.

Tariq had no idea where that appallingly fanciful notion had come from. He would not even be near her now were it not for the mornings he had woken in the palace in Nur, overcome by the feverish need to claim this woman once more. He scowled down at her, and then scowled harder when she only smiled that mysterious smile again in return, unfazed by him.

"Come," he ordered her, at his most autocratic, and took her arm. Not roughly, but not brooking any argument, either, he led her across the terrace and ushered her into the quiet house.

His staff had discreetly lit a few lamps indoors. They cast soft beams of light across the marble floors and against the high, graceful ceilings. He led her through the maze of galleries filled with priceless art and reception rooms crowded with extravagant antiques that comprised a large portion of the highest floor of the house, all of them boasting stellar views of nighttime Paris from the soaring windows. He barely noticed.

"Where are we going?" she asked, but there was a lack of curiosity in her voice. As if she was as cool and as unaffected as she claimed to be, which he could not countenance. Surely it shouldn't matter—surely she could pretend anything she wished and he should not care in the slightest—but Tariq fought to keep himself from growling at her. He could not accept that she was so calm while he felt so wild. Even if her calmness was, as he suspected and wanted to believe, an act.

None of this matters, he reminded himself, coldly. *As long as you get her out of your system, once and for all.*

After all, despite his obsessive concentration on a single woman for far too long, the truth was that Tariq did not have time for this. He had a country to run. Nur was poised on the brink of great change, but change did not come easily, especially in his part of the world. There was always a price. There were always those who preferred to stick to the old ways, out of fear or faith or sheer stubbornness. There were those who wanted only to see the old regime, of which Tariq was the last surviving member, crumble and disappear, and no matter that such a thing would cause even more chaos and bloodshed.

There were border disputes to settle, and tribal councils to oversee. Tariq loved his beautiful, harsh, deeply complicated and often conflicted country more than he had ever loved a human being, including himself. It felt like the worst kind of disloyalty to be tangled up with this woman, especially since she was the last one he had been with in his previous incarnation. Perhaps he judged her more severely because she was the other face he saw when he revisited his old disgraceful behavior in his mind.

Tariq led Jessa into the sumptuous master suite that sprawled across the back of the house, and only released her arm when he had closed the door behind them, shutting them in. Would she still be so brave now that the games were quickly coming to an end? Would she dare to continue this foolishness?

She took a few steps into the room ahead of him, her head slightly bent and her hands clasped in front of her as if she was listening for second thoughts or offering up a prayer. *Too late,* he thought with no little satisfaction. He let his gaze follow the soft indentation of her spine down to the flare of her hips, as the royal-blue dress shimmied in the low lights and seemed to grow brighter in the reflection of the gilt-edged opulence that surrounded them. Tariq was no particular fan of French furniture—he found it too fussy, too liable to collapse beneath his large frame—but he could appreciate the way so much Continental splendor seemed to enhance her natural glow. She turned her head then, looking at him over her shoulder.

It was as if the room smoldered. Tariq thought only of flame, of heat, of burying himself so deeply inside of her that the only thing he'd care about would be the way she gasped his name.

She did not speak. She only watched him, her eyes wide but without apprehension as he closed the distance between them with a few short strides. He reached out and used his hands to trace the parts of her body that his eyes had so recently touched: the soft nape of her neck, the sinuous length of her spine, the mesmerizing place where her hips curved gently into her bottom. He reached down and drew the silky dress up over her legs, slowly, letting the fabric caress her. The room was silent, only the sounds of their breathing and the faint, seductive whisper of fabric moving against flesh. He prolonged the moment, enjoying the way the dress felt in his hands, enjoying more the way her flushed skin felt as he touched her in passing, and then he drew the filmy dress over her head and cast it aside.

She turned to face him then, a flush rising in her cheeks, and he saw her arms move as if she wanted to cover herself or hide from him. She stopped herself, her expression betraying nothing more than a quick blink of her eyes, and dropped her arms back down to her sides.

She stood before him, clad only in a black lace bra that

pushed her breasts toward him, the swell of all that creamy flesh calling his name, begging for his tongue, his hands. Below, she wore nothing save a pair of sheer panties and her wickedly high shoes. She looked like something she was not, or had not been when he knew her, when he had claimed her innocence as his right. She looked decadent. Delicious.

Mine.

"It appears I will have my dessert before my dinner," Tariq said, pushing aside the possessive urge that roared through him. He traced the delicate ridge of her collarbone, dipping into the hollow where her pulse beat hard against her throat. She was like his own private banquet. Just because he had ulterior motives it didn't mean he wasn't prepared to thoroughly enjoy himself.

"Perhaps I want dessert as well," Jessa replied, only the slightest tremor in her voice, as if she was not flushed with color and practically naked before him.

She wanted to be tough. Tariq smiled, released her.

"Then by all means, help yourself."

She swayed toward him, rocking slightly on her feet. It could be the precarious shoes in the deep carpet, though Tariq rather thought it was the same strange hunger that gripped him and made him feel curiously close to unsteady himself. Then her hands were on him, sweeping across the hard planes of his chest, testing the hardy muscles he'd built up after five years of intensive training with his royal guard. A king must be prepared to fight the battles he expected his subjects to fight, Tariq's uncle had always believed. And so Tariq had transformed himself from an idle playboy who visited a fancy spa-like gym merely to maintain a certain trouser size that photographed well, to a warrior capable of lethal combat. He shrugged off his jacket and let it drop to the floor. The expertly tailored concoction barely made a sound as it hit the ground. Jessa did not spare it so much as a glance.

Tariq's eyes narrowed against his own pounding hunger as he let Jessa explore this new, fierce body of his, sliding her palms from his shoulders to his waist to yank his shirt-tails free from his trousers. He watched her pull her seductive lower lip between her teeth as she worried the buttons out of their holes one by one and slowly, torturously, exposed his skin to the slightly cooler air of the suite around them. When she had unbuttoned every button and unhooked his cuff links, she pushed the shirt back on his shoulders so it hung there, exposing his chest to her view.

She let out a long hiss of breath. He could feel it tickle across his skin, arrowing straight to his arousal, making him thicken. He made no move to hide it, only continued to wait, to watch, to see what she would do.

She looked up then, and their gazes clashed together in a manner that seemed as intimate and passionate as the kisses they'd shared before. Tariq moved to speak, but no words came.

He did not expect her to move, her expression taking on a look of intense feminine satisfaction. He reached for her, but she shocked him by leaning forward and placing her hot, open mouth, that wicked courtesan's mouth that had featured prominently in his fantasies since he'd tasted it again this morning, in the valley between his pectoral muscles.

When he swore, he swore in Arabic, Jessa discovered in a distant kind of amusement, and he still sounded every inch a king.

Not that she cared. She could not seem to stop tasting him. She trailed kisses across one hard pectoral plane, then moved to the other, worrying the hard male nipple she found with the tip of her tongue, laughing softly when she heard him groan.

Jessa moved even closer and pushed the soft linen shirt from Tariq's broad shoulders, letting it fall to the floor behind him. His strong, muscled arms came around her, crushing her breasts against his chest and drawing her into the cradle of his thighs. Just like that, they were pressed together, bare skin against bare skin, so that the intrusion of her lacy, delectable bra seemed almost criminal. Heat coiled in her groin and shot through her, making her head spin. She fought to breathe, and wasn't sure she much cared if she could not. She felt his bare skin against hers like an exultation, like memory and fantasy come to life.

She had not felt like this in five long years. She had missed his skin, the addictive heat of him that sizzled through her and left her feeling branded and desperate for more. Her head dropped back of its own volition, and she heard him muttering words she could not understand against the soft flesh of her neck. He used his tongue, his lips, his teeth. He surrounded her, held her, his hands finding her curves and testing them against his palms, stroking and teasing and driving her hunger to fever pitch. And all the while his exciting, overwhelming hardness pressed against the juncture of her thighs, driving her ever closer to senseless capitulation.

This was how it had always been, this rush to madness, to pleasure, to the addictive ecstasy that only Tariq could bring her. She could not get close enough. She could not think straight, and she could not imagine why she would want to. This was how she remembered him, so hard, so male, dominating her so easily, so completely—

Careful! a voice in the back of her mind whispered, panicked. Jessa pulled herself back from the brink of total surrender, blinking to clear the haze of passion from her eyes. It was so easy to lose herself in him. It was much too easy to forget. She raised her head and searched Tariq's expression. His features were hard, fierce and uncompromising as he stared back at her. She felt herself tremble deep inside—warning or *wanting*, she wasn't sure. But it didn't matter. She had been the one to make this decision. She was not weak, malleable, *senseless*. She could call the shots. She would.

"Second thoughts?" His voice was a rasp, thick with passion, and her hips moved against his in unconscious response. His eyes glittered dangerously, nearly black now in the center of the opulent gold-and-blue room.

"None whatsoever," she replied. She eased back from him, aware that he let her do it, let her move slightly in the circle of his embrace.

Holding his gaze with all the defiance she could muster—*I am strong, not weak; I am in charge*—she dropped her hands to his trousers. His hard mouth curved, and he shifted his weight, giving her easier access.

Jessa remembered her horror at exactly this image earlier this same day—her fear that she would far too easily find herself doing what she was about to do. But it was different now, because he was not compelling her to do it. She was not begging him for anything—she was taking what she wanted. He was not orchestrating anything. He was hers to experience as she wished, to make up for all those lonely nights when she would have done anything at all for the chance to touch him again.

She pulled his belt free of its buckle and unbuttoned the top button of his whisper-soft trousers, letting the backs of her fingers revel in the blazing heat of his taut abdomen and the scrape of the coarse hair that surrounded his manhood.

She moved the zipper down slowly, careful to ease it over the hard ridge of his jutting sex, and then she freed him entirely, reaching between them to cup him in her hands.

He muttered something too low to catch, though she thought it was her name.

She could not recall him ever allowing her this kind of unhurried exploration before. Their passion back then had always been too explosive, too all-encompassing. She had never thought to ask for anything. She had been too awash in sensation, too overcome and swept off her feet. She had surrendered to him entirely, body and soul.

But that was the past. Here, now, she caressed his impressive length. He let out a sound too fierce to be a moan. He reached for her, his hands diving once again into the thick mass of her hair and holding her loosely, encouraging her, not correcting her. Jessa ignored him, and concentrated on this most male part of him instead. He was softer here than anywhere else on his rugged warrior's form, like the softest satin stretched across steel. And so much hotter, so hot that she felt an answering heat flood her own sex, and an ache begin to build inside her.

She raised her head up to meet his gaze, while his hands moved to frame her face. She frowned slightly when he bent his head toward hers. He paused, his mouth a scant breath away. Jessa felt her heart pound and could feel him stir in her hands.

"No?" he asked softly. He did not quite frown in return. "Is this another game, Jessa?"

"This is my night." She felt his hands flex slightly, but she felt too powerful to allow him to cow her. "My game."

"Is that so?" His eyes mocked her, though his expression otherwise remained the same. He did not believe she could take control, perhaps. Or he knew how close she came to losing herself, her head, when he touched her. Jessa told herself it didn't matter.

"Perhaps you should tell me the rules of this game, before you begin it." His voice and his eyes were more distant, suddenly, but his hands against the delicate skin of her cheekbones were still warm, still exciting.

"There is only one rule," Jessa said evenly. Deliberately, so there could be no misunderstanding. "And it is that I am in charge."

Something ignited in his gaze then, and sent an answering shudder down along her spine to weaken her knees. He pulled himself up without seeming to move, arrogant and imperial, and looked at her as if he could not comprehend what she had said. Jessa held her breath.

"And what does that entail, exactly?" he asked, his voice lower and laced with warning. "Will I wake to find myself bound naked from the chandelier, to be tittered over and eventually cut down by the housekeeper?"

Jessa tested out the image of Tariq so completely at her mercy and smiled slightly, even as a hectic kind of restlessness washed through her, urging her to continue what her hands had already started. She tested his length against her palm once again and watched his arrogant focus shatter.

"If that is what I want, then yes," she said recklessly. "Don't pretend you won't enjoy it."

"And what about what I want?" he asked. Idly, he wrapped a single long, copper curl around his finger and tugged. Jessa did not mistake the sensual menace underlying his tone. She shrugged.

"What about it?" she asked.

"Jessa—"

But he cut himself off, because Jessa sank down in front of him, onto her knees, in a single smooth motion. She heard his breath leave him in a rush. She watched his eyes darken even further, becoming like night.

She did not feel diminished. She did not feel mindless or senseless, or under his power. Quite the opposite.

She felt like a goddess.

"Jessa," he said again, but this time her name was a prayer. A wish.

She smiled. And then she took him deep into her mouth.

CHAPTER EIGHT

JESSA heard him sigh, or maybe he said her name once more, too low to be heard.

It was thrilling. Jessa felt her own sex throb and melt in time to his slow, careful thrusts, and felt him grow harder. He moaned and she felt potent. Alive. Powerful beyond imagining.

"Enough," he said suddenly, abruptly disengaging from her.

Jessa sat back on her heels, stunned.

"I'm the one who will decide when it's enough," she retorted, glaring up at him. "Not you. Or have you already forgotten that I'm to be in charge?"

"I have not forgotten anything," Tariq replied, his voice clipped, rough, impatient with need. "But perhaps you have forgotten that I did not agree."

"But you—"

"Later," Tariq said, interrupting her. He sank to his knees on the carpet in front of her, making her heart stutter in her chest before kicking into a frenetic beat. This close, Jessa could see the wildness in his eyes, and the passion stamped across his features, giving him a certain breathtaking ferocity.

She started to argue, but instead he leaned closer and claimed her mouth with his. He held her head between his hands, held her captive, and she didn't think to fight it. He moved her to the angle that best suited him, plundering her mouth with his, taking control. Claiming her. Proving his mastery, and it made her ache and swell and melt against him. Again. Then again, and again.

Heat like liquid washed over her, through her. She felt hectic, frantic, alive with need, shaky from the inside out. She buried her hands in his thick, black hair, exulting in the way it felt like rough silk against her palms, in such contrast to the punishing, glorious demands of his mouth.

It occurred to Jessa that she should protest, wrench back the control she refused to accept he'd only allowed her, indulged her.

Tariq took one strong, capable hand from her head and slid it down her back, leaving trails of sensation in his wake, causing her to arch against him at the wonder of his touch. Then he moved around to her front and pulled once, twice, against the band of her panties. By the time Jessa registered the fact that he was using both of his hands, and that he seemed to be tugging, there was a rip and he was done. He tossed her torn panties aside, and the look he slanted her way dared her to comment on it.

She didn't say a word. She wasn't sure she could speak. She was having trouble breathing, much less thinking, as they knelt together in the center of the thick Aubusson carpet.

Tariq's long, elegant fingers slipped between her thighs, tracing the contours of her sex, then the honeyed heat within. His green eyes held her still, imprisoned her, even as he tested her tight sheath with one strong finger, then another. Jessa felt herself clench around him, and shuddered.

"Forgive me, but I cannot wait for you to finish playing

your games with me," he said then, but there was absolutely no apology in the way he looked at her. He was all arrogant male, every inch a king, and he did not wait for her to respond. Instead, he slid his hands back up the length of her torso and then picked her up as if she weighed no more than a pound coin. He shifted her across the space between them and settled her astride him.

"Tariq—" But she didn't know what she wanted to say, or how to say it, and he merely twisted his hips and thrust deep inside her.

So deep. So full. Finally.

"Yes," he said, need pulling his face taut, his eyes black and wild for her. "Finally."

Only then did Jessa realize she'd spoken aloud. Her breasts seemed to swell even more against their prison of lace, and she rubbed herself helplessly against the wall of his chest, unable to stop, unable to get enough of the feel of him. Again. *Finally.*

The perfection of it, of him, of their bodies fused together, overwhelmed her. She had no memory of looping her arms around his neck, and yet she held him. Other memories, older ones, of the many times they'd tested the feverish joy of this slick, matchless, breathtaking union, threatened to spill from her eyes.

Now she remembered why she had thrown away her life so heedlessly because of this man. Now she remembered why she had let Tariq twist her into knots and cast her aside like a rag doll—why she hadn't even recognized what was happening until it was done. For the glory of this moment, this connection, this addictive, electrifying link.

And then he moved, one long, sure stroke, and Jessa came apart. He thrust once, twice. She sobbed against him while her body exploded into pieces, as she shook and shook and shook. She panted, her face in the crook of his neck. The world disappeared and there was nothing but the singular scent and taste of Tariq's skin at her mouth, and his hard length still buried deep in her sex.

"Come back to me." His voice was rough, intimate. "Now." It was no less an order for the sensual tone in which it was delivered. Still, it made her shiver.

"I am finished," she managed to say, her eyes still closed, her head still cradled between his throat and his wide shoulder. She meant, *I am dead.* She was not sure she would have minded were that true.

"But I am not." Tariq shifted position, holding her bottom in one large hand and keeping her hips flush with his. "Hold on to me," he demanded, and she was too dazed, too drunk on the sensations still firing through her to do anything but what he asked. She wrapped her arms around his shoulders and then everything whirled around and she was on her back on the plush carpet and he was between her legs and still so deep inside her, so hard and so big, she thought she might weep from the sheer pleasure of it.

Tariq bent his head and took a stiff nipple into his mouth, sucking on it through the lace barrier. Jessa moaned as a new fire seared through her, the slight abrasion of the lace and the hot, wet heat of his mouth together almost too much to bear.

He laughed softly, and began to move his hips, guiding himself in and out of her with consummate, devastating skill. He turned his attention to her other breast, making Jessa arch into him again and raise her hips to meet his every stroke. Their hips moved in perfect harmony. Once again, she ached. Once again, the fire grew and raged and consumed her. Jessa felt the storm growing within her, taking her to fever pitch, though she fought against it.

"Let go," he said, his voice fierce, his gaze intense.

"But you—and I—" But how could she concentrate on what she wanted to say when every slide of his body against hers turned her molten, incandescent?

"I command it," he said.

Her eyes flew wide. Tariq smiled. And then he reached between their bodies and touched her, and she flew over the edge again.

This time, he did not stop. He did not wait. He continued to thrust into her, slow and steady, until her sobs became ragged breaths and her eyes focused once more on his face.

"One more time," he ordered her, his eyes gleaming.

"I cannot possibly!"

"You can." He bent toward her, pulling the lace cup away from one breast to tease the flesh beneath with his lips. His tongue. His teeth. Jessa shuddered in response. Tariq slanted a look at her. "You will."

And when she did, he went with her.

It took a long time for Jessa to return to earth, and when she did, he was still stretched out over her, still pressing her into the floor. She was afraid to think too much about what had just happened. She was afraid to allow herself to face it. She wasn't certain she would like what she might find.

That much pleasure could only be trouble. She could not assign it too much meaning, decide it was something it could never be. She could not allow herself to forget that this was her idea. That she was here to take some of this pleasure for herself and hoard it. This was her long-overdue goodbye, that was all. She didn't know why she felt so fragile, so vulnerable.

Tariq stirred and rolled off her, sitting up as he yanked his trousers back into place. As he fastened them, Jessa struggled to sit up herself. Was this it, then? She hadn't thought much beyond the actual pleasure part of the *one night of pleasure* idea. How was one expected to negotiate such moments? The last time she had been with him, she had been openly and happily in love with him. There had been no awkwardness. Jessa pulled her bra back into position, and swallowed when her eyes fell on the torn scraps of what used to be her panties. She looked down and saw, with some amazement, that she still wore her imprac-tical shoes.

Beside her, Tariq rose to his feet in a single, lithe movement that reminded her that he was a warrior now, in ways she could only pretend to understand. He turned and looked down at her, his expression unreadable.

Jessa was suddenly painfully aware of her surroundings, the majestic grandeur of the well-appointed room, from its carved moldings to the graceful furniture that looked more like works of art than places to sit or to store belongings. It was not even the bedroom, merely the first in what she could see now was a series of rooms. A suite, complete with floor-to-ceiling windows that showed off the lights of Paris shooting off in all directions. Tariq stood before her, half-naked, his thick hair tangled and hanging around his face, making him look untamed and remote but no less regal. He belonged in such a place, surrounded by such things. And here she was, half-naked on a priceless rug, Jessa Heath from Fulford with nothing to show for herself, not even her panties.

It occurred to her that he had only said he wanted to get her out of his system. He had never elaborated what might happen when he had.

The moment stretched between them, long past awkward. Jessa could still feel him between her legs, and yet it was as if a perfect stranger stood before her, carved from stone. Some avenging angel prepared to hand down judgment.

But she had been through worse, she reminded herself,

and no matter what happened, no matter how unpleasant the moment, she had chosen this. That was the key point. She had *chosen* this.

Jessa sat up straighter and pushed her hair back from her face. It hardly mattered if she looked disheveled at this point, after all. He must have had his mouth or his hands on every inch of her body. And what could he possibly do or say to her? Would he leave her cruelly, perhaps? She had already survived that once, relatively unscathed. She met his gaze proudly.

"Thank you," she said in her most polite tone. It was the one she used in fancy restaurants and to bank managers. "That was exactly what I wanted."

"I am delighted to hear it." His tone was sardonic. "I live to serve." Now he openly mocked her. She pretended she could not hear the edge in his voice.

"Yes, well." She got to her feet with rather less grace than he had displayed, and looked around for her dress. She saw it in a crumpled heap a few feet away. "If only that were true. You would be a different man, wouldn't you?" She moved toward the dress.

"Jessa." Her name was another command, and she looked at him even though she knew she should ignore him, pick up her things and walk out. "What are you doing?"

"My dress…" She gestured at it but couldn't seem to turn away from him, not when he was looking at her that way, so brooding and dark and something else, something she might have called possessive on another man.

"You won't need it."

"I won't?"

He didn't move, he only watched her, but his eyes were hot. Jessa was shocked to feel her body respond to him. Anew. Again. Her nipples hardened, her sex pulsed.

It was absurd. She had gotten what she'd wanted, hadn't she? What was the point of drawing it out? No matter how ravenous she seemed to be for him.

"We are not done here," he said quietly. His gaze was hard, yet she softened. "We have hardly begun."

CHAPTER NINE

TARIQ stood at the window that rose high above the bedroom, looking out over the city. Dawn snuck in with long pink fingers, teasing the famous rooftops of Paris before him, yet he barely saw it. Behind him, Jessa slept in the great bed that stood in the center of the ornate room, the heavy white-and-gold-brocade coverlet long since discarded, her naked limbs curled beneath her, rose and pink from the exertions of the long night. He did not need to confirm this with his own eyes again; he would hear it if her breathing altered, if she turned over, if she awoke.

It was as if he could feel her body as an extension of his own. Perhaps this was inevitable after such a night, he told himself, but he knew better. He had lived a life of excess for more years than he cared to recall, and he had had many nights that would qualify as extreme, and yet he had never felt this kind of connection to a woman. He didn't care for it. It reminded him of all the things he had worked so hard to forget.

"You make me feel alive," he had told her once, years ago, recklessly, and she had laughed as she rose above him, naked and beautiful, her face open and filled with light.

"You *are* alive," she had whispered in his ear, holding him close. She had then proceeded to prove it to them both.

Tariq had lost count of the times he had reached for her last night, or her for him. He knew he had slept but little, far more interested in tasting her, teasing her, sinking into her one more time. He had reacquainted himself with every nook and cranny of her body, all of its changes, all of its secrets—the pleasure so intense, so astounding, that he could not bring himself to let it end.

Because he knew that once he stopped, he would have to face the truths he was even now avoiding. And as the night wore on, Tariq had found himself less and less interested in doing so.

"This is a feast," Jessa had said at some point, while they sat in the sitting room and ate some of the rich food they'd ignored earlier, wearing very little in the way of clothes. She had smiled at him, unselfconscious and at ease with her legs folded beneath her and her hair tumbled down around her bare shoulders. She had looked free. Just as she had always been with him.

"Indeed it is," he had replied, but he had not been talking about the meal.

Memories chased through him now, hurtling him back to a time he wanted to forget—had worked to forget, in fact, for years. Touching her, tasting her, breathing in her scent. These things had unlocked something in him that he had worked hard to keep hidden, even from himself.

His parents had died in a car accident when he was too young to remember more than fleeting images of his father's rare smile, his mother's dark curtain of hair. He had been taken into the palace by his only remaining relative, his uncle the king, and raised with his cousins, the princes of Nur. His uncle was the only parent Tariq had ever known, and yet Tariq had always been keenly aware that he was not his uncle's son. Just as he had always known that his cousins were the future rulers of the country, and had been trained from birth as such.

"Your cousins have responsibilities to our people," his uncle had told Tariq when they were all still young.

"And what are my responsibilities?" Tariq had asked guilelessly.

His uncle had only smiled at him and patted him on the head.

Tariq had understood. He was not important, not in the way his cousins were.

And so he did as he pleased. Though his uncle periodically suggested that Tariq had more to offer the world than a life full of expensive cars and equally costly European models, Tariq had never seen the point in discovering what that was. He had played with the stock market because it amused him and he was good at it, but it had been no more to him than another kind of high-stakes poker game like the ones he played in private back rooms in Monte Carlo.

He had long since buried the feelings that had haunted him as a child—that he was an outcast in his own family, tolerated by them yet never of them. He believed they cared for him, but he knew he was their charity case. Their duty. Never simply theirs.

Tariq heard Jessa move in the bed behind him. He turned to see if she had awoken and if it was time at last to have a conversation he had no wish to pursue. But she only settled herself into a different position, letting out a small, contented sigh.

He turned back around to face the window, heedless of the cool air on his bare skin, still caught up in the past. The summer he had met Jessa was the summer his uncle had finally put his foot down. He could not threaten Tariq with the loss of his income or possessions, of course, for Tariq had quadrupled his own personal fortune by that point, and then some. But that did not mean the old man had been without weapons.

"You must change your life," the old king had said, frowning at Tariq across the table set out for them on the balcony high on the cliffs. He had summoned his nephew to the family villa on their private island in the Mediterranean, off the coast of Turkey, for this conversation. Tariq had not expected it to be pleasant, though he had always managed to talk his uncle out of his tempers in the past. He had assumed he would do the same that day.

"Into what?" Tariq had asked, shrugging, watching the waves rise and fall far below them, deep and blue. He had been thirty-four then and so world-weary. So profoundly bored. "My life is the envy of millions."

"Your life is empty," his uncle had retorted. "Meaningless." He waved his hand in disgust, taking in Tariq's polished, too fashionable appearance. "What are you but one more playboy sheikh, looked down upon by the entire world, confirming all their worst suspicions about our people?"

"Until they want my money," Tariq had replied coolly. "At which point it is amazing how quickly they become respectful. Even obsequious."

"And this is enough for you? This is all you aspire to? You, who carry the royal blood of the kingdom of Nur in your veins?"

"What would you have me do, Uncle?" Tariq had asked, impatient though he dared not show it. They had had this conversation, or some version of it, every year since Tariq had gone to university where, to his uncle's dismay, he had not approached his studies with the same level of commitment he had shown when approaching the women in his classes.

"You do nothing," his uncle had said matter-of-factly, in a more serious tone than Tariq had ever heard from him, at least when directed at Tariq personally. "You play games with money and call it a career, but it is a joke. You win, you lose, it is all a game to you. You are an entirely selfish creature. I would tell you to marry, to do your duty to your family and your bloodline as your cousins must do, but what would you have to offer your sons? You are barely a man."

Tariq had gritted his teeth. This was not just his uncle talking, not just the only version of a parent he had ever known—this was his king. He had no choice but to tolerate it.

"Again," he had managed to say eventually, fighting to keep his tone appropriately respectful, "what is it you want me to do?"

"It is not about what I want," his uncle had said, disappointment dripping from every hard word. "It is about who you are. I cannot force you to do anything. You are not my son. You are not my heir."

He could not have known, Tariq had supposed then, how deeply his words cut, how close to the bone. No matter that they were no more than the truth.

"But you will no longer be welcome in my family unless you contribute to it in some way," his uncle had continued. He had stared at Tariq for a moment, his eyes grim. "You have six months to prove this to me. If you have not changed your ways by then, I will wash my hands of you." He had shaken his head. "And I must tell you, nephew, I am not hopeful."

Tariq had left the villa that same night, determined to put distance between himself and his uncle and the words his uncle had said, at last vocalizing Tariq's worst fears.

He was not a son, an heir. He was disposable. He was no more than a duty, dictated by tradition and law. But he was not family in a way that mattered. He shared nothing with them but blood. Whatever that meant.

Tariq had never been so angry, so at sea, in all of his life. He had never felt so alienated and alone, and he was not a man who had ever formed deep attachments, so he had not known how to handle what was, he thought in retrospect, grief.

And then he had met Jessa, and she had loved him.

He knew that she had loved him, instantly and thoroughly. She had charmed him with the force of her adoration and her artlessness—her inability to conceal it, or play sophisticated games. Other women had fallen in love with him before, or so they had claimed, but had they loved Tariq or his bank balance? He had never cared before. He had lied about who he was, angrily attempting to distance himself from his reputation as if that might appease his uncle, but she had not noticed.

"You trust too easily," he had told her one night, when they lay stretched out before the fire, unable to stop touching each other.

"I do not!" she had protested, laughing at him, her face tilted toward him, her eyes warm and soft, like cinnamon sugar. "I am quite savvy!"

"If you say so," he had murmured, playing with her curls, coiling them around his fingers. At first he had waited for her to change, as they all did once they learned who he was. He had waited for those knowing looks, or the clever feminine ways of asking for money, or a new car, or an apartment in a posh neighborhood. But Jessa had never changed. She had simply loved him.

"I trust *you*, Tariq," she had whispered then, still smiling. She had even kissed him, with all the innocence and passion she had in her young body.

When she looked at him with those wide cinnamon eyes that reminded him of the home he wasn't sure he would ever be permitted to see again, he felt like the man he should have been.

But then she had disappeared abruptly and completely, which had bothered him far more than it should have. And before he could make sense of what he felt, his uncle and cousins had died, all at once, and Tariq had been forced to face reality. What was the love of one besotted girl when there were wars to prevent and a country to run and those last, terrible words from his uncle that he could never disprove? He could never show his uncle that he was, in fact, a man. That he, too, could uphold the family honor and do his duty. That he had only ever wanted to be treated as a part of the family in the first place.

He turned then, letting his gaze fall upon the sinuous curves of her body as she lay on her side, facing away from him, the curve of her hip and the dip of her waist even more enticing now, after he had had her in every way he could imagine. He had meant only to slake his desire, to have her and be done with her at last. He had spent years convincing himself that she was no more than an itch that needed to be scratched. He had not expected to feel anything but lust.

He had convinced himself he would *feel* nothing at all.

"You are a fool," he whispered to himself.

But Jessa Heath still managed to cast a spell around him. It was the way she gave herself over with total abandon, he thought, studying her form in the morning light. To her anger, to her passion.

Even now that she knew exactly who he was, she still

wanted nothing from him. If anything, his real identity made her like him less. And yet she still fell to pieces in his arms, shattered at the slightest touch. It was as if she had been made specifically for him. As if she could still make him that man she'd seen in him five years ago, as if he was that man, finally, when he was with her.

Which was why he let her sleep, why he crossed the room and sat beside her, drinking her in, knowing that once she woke, the spell would be broken. Reality would intrude once again and remind him that he needed a queen, and she was the girl who had become the emblem of his disappointing former life.

And this night would become one more fever dream, one more memory, that he would lock away and soon enough, he knew, forget.

Jessa woke slowly.

The morning sun poured in from the tall windows, illuminating the bed and making her feel as if she was lit from within. She tugged the tangled length of her hair out from beneath her, knowing it had to be wild after such a night. Knowing she was wild and raw inside as well, though she couldn't think about it. Not yet. Not quite yet.

Not while he was still so near.

She knew he was there before she saw him, as if she had an internal radar that told her Tariq's specific whereabouts. She turned her head and there he was, just where she had sensed him. He sat on the edge of the bed, still gloriously naked, his body like something that ought to be carved in the finest marble and displayed in museums. He was not looking at her for the moment, so Jessa let herself drink her fill of him.

Something in the way he held himself, the way he stared

broodingly toward the window, made her frown. He looked almost sad. She wanted to reach over and soothe him, to kiss away whatever darkness had come upon him while she slept. She might not know *why* he wanted her as he had told her he did from the first, but she had come to accept that it was true, over and over again in the night. The wonder was, she wanted him too. Still. Even now.

But then he turned his head. His expression was unreadable, his dark green eyes solemn, his dark hair the kind of tousled mess that begged to be touched. Though she did not dare.

It was only to be expected that things should feel strained, Jessa reflected, staring back at him for a moment. One night, they had both said. And now it was morning, and the sun was too bright, and it was best to put all of this behind them.

She would not think about what they had done or the ways they had done it. She would not think about how she had sobbed and cried out for him and screamed his name. Again and again and again. It was only sex, she told herself sternly. Just sex. No need to torture herself about it. No need to give her emotions free rein, no matter how much her heart wanted her to do otherwise. She could be more like a man and compartmentalize. Why not? Sex was simply sex. It had nothing to do with feelings unless one wished otherwise. And she did not wish it. End of story.

Now he could go his way and she hers. Just as they had planned. There was no need to dig any further into their past and haul all of that pain back into the light of day. It could be boxed up and locked away, forever.

She remembered that she was supposed to feel empowered, not suddenly shy, no matter how exposed she felt.

"So," she said, trying to sound matter-of-fact. "It is finally morning."

"So it is." Tariq did not move, he only watched her. It was unnerving. Her heart began to pick up speed, though she was not sure why.

"I can't help but notice that I am in France," Jessa said, looking beyond him to the graceful Paris streets outside the window. She had always meant to visit Paris. She wasn't certain this counted. "Rather farther away from York than I expected to be. I hope you will not mind—"

"Jessa."

She flushed, suddenly furious, or that was what she called the emotion that flashed through her, hot and dangerous. She made a fist and struck the soft bedding beside her.

"I hate it when you do that," she threw at him. "You do not have to interrupt me all the time. I don't care if you're a king. You are not *my* king. It's just rude."

"And, of course, I would not wish to appear rude," Tariq replied, an edge in his voice that made the fine hairs on the back of her neck stand up straight. "I have made you come more times than you can possibly count, and you wish to lecture me on—"

"How do you like it?" she demanded, interrupting him. "It's frustrating, isn't it? Because, obviously, the person interrupting believes that whatever he has to say is of far more importance, that *he* is of far more importance—"

"Or perhaps the person talking is overwrought and hysterical." His voice was cool. Jessa bit her lip and looked away. She became uncomfortably aware of her own nudity, and of the fact that the frustrated heat in her cheeks was no doubt evident all over her exposed body.

She knew what she was doing. She was drawing this out, deliberately avoiding any number of elephants in the room. Another way to do that was simply to leave. The agreed-upon night was over and done. There was no more reason for them to be talking about anything. He had claimed what he wanted, as had she, and her secrets remained safe. It was time instead to return to her life and finally put Tariq where he belonged—in the past.

It was long past time to move on.

She swung her legs to the edge of the bed and stood, not looking at him.

"I think I'll take a bath," she said. She had never sounded so chipper, so polite. "Then I need to return to York."

She felt awkward. Tense. Perhaps that was just how she would continue to feel until she was safely back in her own life. She tried to shake it off. But when she started to move toward the bathroom, a luxurious palace all its own, she had to walk in front of him, and he held up a hand.

"Come here," he said quietly.

She hesitated, but then reminded herself that she had already handled him. She had already made it through the night intact. What could he do now? She had made love to him so many times that she'd forgotten anything existed outside of him, and yet she had still woken up herself. Whole, complete. Not lost in him as she had been before. So why was she this nervous?

She moved toward him, wary. It was something about the look in his eyes, something she couldn't place. Not that dark passion he seemed to fight against as much as she did. Not lust. She was more than familiar with those. He beckoned for her to come closer, inside the vee of his powerful legs. Cautiously, she complied.

He did not look up at her. He raised his hands and placed them on her hips, lightly encircling them. His fingers smoothed against her skin, tracing patterns from her hipbone to her navel, then back. Bemused, and not unaffected by his touch, even now, Jessa blinked down at him.

He looked up then and, as their gazes met, Jessa suddenly knew with searing, gut-wrenching certainty exactly what he was doing.

Her breath deserted her in a rush.

Tariq was not touching her randomly. He was not caressing her. He was tracing the faint white lines that scored her belly—the stretch marks she had tried to rub away with lotions and creams, the lines more visible now in the bright morning light than she remembered them ever being before. They were the unmistakable evidence that she had been pregnant—enormously pregnant.

The world stopped turning. Her heart stopped beating. His eyes bored into her as his hands tightened. She heard only white noise, a rushing in her ears, and everything else went blank as if she had lost consciousness for a moment, though she was not so lucky.

He only waited.

And then, when he had stared at her so long she was convinced he had ripped every last secret from her very soul, his mouth twisted.

She wanted to speak—to yell, to defend herself, to deny everything—but it was as if she were paralyzed. Frozen solid, watching her world end in his dark green gaze, colder now than she had ever seen it. He held her still, his captive, and when he spoke, his voice held so much suspicion, so much accusation, she flinched.

"I have only one question for you," he said, every word like a knife. "Where is the child?"

CHAPTER TEN

EVERY instinct screamed at Jessa to run, to escape, to do anything in her power to put space between herself and the knowledge she saw dawning in his eyes.

But she could not bring herself to move.

"Well?" he asked, his voice like a gunshot. "Have you had a child, Jessa?" His voice dropped to the barest whisper of sound as he searched her face. He actually paled, his eyes widening as he read her expression. "Have you had *my* child?"

Her mind whirled as panic flooded through her, cramping her stomach and making little black spots appear before her eyes. She could feel herself waver as she stood before him. *Think!* she ordered herself. She had never planned to see him again, and once he had appeared, had had no plan to tell him about Jeremy. Why should she? She had expected him to disappear again. What good could come of dredging up a past neither one of them could change?

She hadn't expected to be confronted with that past in so dramatic a manner. She was completely unprepared!

Tariq might suspect that Jeremy existed. But he didn't know who Jeremy was, or *where* he was. Only Jessa could protect Jeremy from Tariq and the devastation that would inevitably rain down on Jeremy's world—because Jessa knew without a shadow of a doubt that if Tariq knew where Jeremy was, Tariq would do everything in his considerable power to take him back. And so she would do what she had to do, no matter what it cost her. She would protect Jeremy, even from Tariq.

"I asked you a question," Tariq said, his harsh tone slicing into her, making her jump again. "Do not make me repeat it."

Jessa sucked in a breath. His fingers were like vises, clamped on to her hips and chaining her in place, though he had not increased the pressure of his hands against her flesh. She didn't know how she managed to keep from collapsing, as her heart galloped inside her chest. *Think of Jeremy,* she told herself. *You must be brave for him.*

"I heard you," she said, fear making her voice sound clipped. It was better than terrified. "I just don't have any idea what you're talking about."

His lips pressed together, and he released her suddenly, surging to his feet. Jessa scrambled away from him, determined to put as much space as she could between them. She moved around the end of the huge bed, pulling the decadently soft top sheet from the mattress and wrapping it around herself. She could not bear to remain naked in front of him, not for one second more. She could have kicked herself for failing to remember that her own body could betray her in this way. But she hadn't paid attention to her stretch marks in ages. They were simply there, a part of her personal landscape she noticed as much as she noticed her knees or her ankles. She was such a fool! But then, she had also thought that she could seduce and control Tariq. What had she been thinking?

He did not have to follow her—he loomed over her

from the other side of the bed, his arms crossed over his powerful chest, his anger making him seem even larger than before. He did not seem to care that he, too, was naked. He was as intimidating now as he was when fully dressed. More, perhaps.

"Is that how you want to play this?" he asked, his eyes dark with outrage. As if he had never whispered her name in passion or cradled her against that hard chest as they each fought for breath. "Do you think it will work?"

"I think you're insane!" she threw at him. She had to get over the shock of this change, this about-face from lover to accuser, and she had to do it immediately, no matter her feelings. Or he would roll right over her and take what he wanted. Of that, she had no doubt.

"Do you think I am a fool?" He shook his head slightly, every muscle in his body tensed. His fury was a palpable thing, another presence in the room, a syrupy cloud between them. "I can see the changes in your body with my own eyes. How do you explain them?"

"It's called *five years!*" she cried, throwing up the hand that did not hold the sheet, letting it show her exasperation, hoping he could not see her terror, her desperation. "I have not pointed out the numerous ways *your* body is not the same as it was when you were five years younger—"

Cold and hard, his gaze slammed into her with the force of a blow, and cut her off that effectively.

"I can tell that you are lying," Tariq said, each word distinct and clear. Like separate bullets fired from the same weapon. "Do you doubt it? Your whole face has changed. You look like a stranger! Where is the child? I saw no sign of one in your home."

Still reeling, Jessa clung to the part that mattered most—he could not know anything about Jeremy specifically. He only knew that Jeremy *could* exist. He had not known about Jeremy before he'd come to York. This was all an accident, her fault.

"You will not even answer the question?" he asked, as if he could not quite believe it. "Your body makes you a liar, Jessa. The time for hiding is over." He was not her lover now. Not the charming, easygoing one she knew now had never been more than a convenient costume for him, and not the intensely sensual one who had taken her to erotic heights last night. His voice was crisp. Relentless. Sure. He was a king with absolute power, and he was not afraid to use it.

"Have you seen me with a child?" she asked coolly, praying he could not see how her hands clenched to white knuckles, or hear the tremor in her voice.

"I will rip your life apart, piece by piece, until I find the truth," Tariq bit out, the supreme monarch handing down his judgment, his eyes blazing. "There is no place you can hide, no part of your life you can keep from me. Is that what you want?"

"Why even ask me what I want?" she said, fear and determination a cold knot in her gut, forcing her to play the part of someone far more brave, far more courageous, than she could ever be. For Jeremy, she could keep from falling apart, falling to pieces, as was no doubt Tariq's goal. For Jeremy, she could fight back. "You did not ask me what I wanted when you abandoned me and ruined my life five years ago. You did not ask me what I wanted when you reappeared in my life. Why pretend you have any interest in what I want now?" She shrugged, meeting his eyes with a brazen courage she did not feel. "If you want to dig around in my life, go right ahead. What could I do to stop you?"

His scowl deepened. "Do you think I am still playing games with you?" he demanded, his voice getting louder, his accent growing more pronounced as his temper grew. "You have no right to keep my child from me! The heir to my kingdom!"

Jessa reminded herself that he did not know. He only suspected. *He did not know.*

"You have no right to speak to me this way!" she retorted.

"Where is the child?" he thundered.

But she couldn't back down, though her knees felt like jelly and her lungs constricted painfully. She wouldn't tell him anything.

The truth was, she hardly knew where to start.

She shook her head, too many emotions fighting for space inside of her, and all of them too messy, too complicated, too heavy.

"Jessa." This time the anger was gone, and something far more like desperation colored his voice. "You must tell me what happened. You must."

But she could not speak another word, and she could not bring herself to look at him. She had the sense that she had finally stopped running a very long, very arduous race, and the wind was knocked out of her.

She didn't have the slightest idea what to do now. She had never so much as considered the possibility that Tariq might discover that he had fathered a child. The time for telling him had long since passed, and she knew that she had tried then, to no avail. She had never anticipated that he might return. She had stopped dreaming such foolish dreams long ago.

And now he stared at her in anguish, which she would give anything to fix and couldn't. It wasn't simply that she couldn't bring herself to tell him what he wanted to know. She physically could not seem to form the words. She could not even think them. She could only lie and avoid and deflect. She could only make it worse.

"I will stop at nothing to locate a child of my blood," Tariq said softly. There was a chilling finality to his words then, as if he was making a vow. He took a step toward her, and it took everything she had to stand her ground before him. "I have believed I am the last of my blood, my family, for five years, Jessa. The very last. If that is not so…"

He didn't finish. But then, he did not have to finish.

Jessa still could not speak. It was as if everything inside her had shut down, turned off.

"You can only remain silent for so long," he said. His voice was like a whip, cracking through the room hard enough to leave welts against her skin. "But do not doubt that there is only one outcome to this situation. I *will* find out. The only question is how much of your life I will destroy in the process."

"Do not bully me!" she cried, surprising herself as well as him, the words ripping from her as if she had torn them from her heart.

"You think I am bullying you?" He was incredulous, pronouncing *bullying* as if he had never heard the term before.

"Threats, intimidation." Jessa pressed one hand against her temple. "Is there another word for it?"

"I am not threatening you, Jessa," he said matter-of-factly, with that ruthlessness underneath. "I am telling you exactly what will happen to you if you continue this. You have no right to keep the truth from me. These are promises."

"What kind of man are you?" she whispered. She wasn't sure why she said it. She wanted to sob, to scream, to somehow release the tension that felt as if it swelled up from inside her.

Their eyes locked across the few feet that separated them. He looked as if he had never seen her before, as if she was a perfect stranger who had wounded him. She realized in that moment that she never wanted to be responsible for his pain. That it hurt her, too. But understanding only made the riot inside swirl faster, swell harder, cause more damage. Jessa made herself hold his gaze, though it cost her.

Tariq looked away from her then, as if he had to collect himself before he did something he would regret.

"I suggest you rethink your position," he said quietly.

Suddenly her tongue was loose. And foolish. "I suggest you—"

"Silence!" He slashed a hand through the air, and said something in what she assumed was Arabic. "I am done listening to you."

He did not look at her again, but strode toward the bedroom door. Jessa could not believe it. Relief flooded through her. He was *leaving?* That was it? Could she really be that lucky?

And what was the part of her that yearned, despite everything, for him to stay?

"Where are you going?" she asked, because she wanted to confirm it.

"Shocking as it might seem to you, I have matters of state to attend to," he growled at her. "Or do you think my kingdom should grind to a halt while you spin your little lies? You can consider this conversation postponed."

"I am not going to sit around and calmly wait for you to come back and be even more horrible to me," she told him fiercely. "I am going home."

He turned when he reached the door to the rest of the suite, his eyes narrow and his mouth hard.

"By all means," he said, his voice as dark as his gaze, and his warning clear, "go wherever you like. See what happens when you do." Then he turned his back on her, seemingly still unconcerned with his nudity, and strode from the room.

His sudden absence left a black hole in the room that Jessa feared might suck her in, for a dizzy, irrational beat or two of her heart. For long moments, Jessa could not move. She told herself she was waiting to see if Tariq would return. She told herself she was merely being cautious. But the truth was that she could not have moved so much as an inch if her life depended upon it.

Eventually, when he did not come back, Jessa moved to the edge of the bed and sat down gingerly, carefully, unable to process what had just occurred. Unable to track the course of the past two days. She remembered going to work in the letting agency that morning, having no idea that her whole world would be turned on its ear. That normal, everyday morning felt as far away to her now as if it belonged to someone else, as if it were a part of some other woman's life. She felt as if she'd just been tipped from a roller coaster at its height and sent tumbling to the earth. She raised a hand to her mouth, surprised to find her hand shook.

She almost let out a sob, but choked it back. She could not break down. She was not safe from Tariq or his questions simply because he had left her alone for the moment. He would be back. She knew that as surely as she knew the earth still turned beneath her feet. He was an implacable force, and she did not know how she had failed to recognize that five years ago. Hadn't she known this would happen? Wasn't this why she'd set upon this course in the first place, to divert his attention?

That is not the only reason… a traitorous voice whispered, but she couldn't allow herself to listen to it. Nor could she savor the heated images of the night before. None of that mattered now.

Jeremy is his child too, the same treacherous voice

whispered, and Jessa felt a wave of old grief rock through her then, nearly knocking her over with all the strength of what might have been. If he had been who he'd said he was. If she had been less infatuated and less silly. If his uncle had not died. If she had been able to care for her newborn child as he deserved to be cared for. *If.*

She balled her hands into fists and stood, ignoring her trembling knees, her shallow breaths, the insistent dampness in her eyes that she refused to let flow free. Tariq would be back, and she did not want to imagine what new ammunition he would bring with him. She was not at all sure she could survive another encounter like this one. In truth, she was not even certain she *had* survived. Not intact, anyway.

But she couldn't think of that, of what more she might have lost. She told herself she had to think of Jeremy. She could take care of herself later.

She had to make certain that whenever Tariq returned, she was long gone.

CHAPTER ELEVEN

IT WAS not until Jessa arrived at the Gare de Lyon railway station with every intention of escaping Tariq—and France—that she realized, with a shock, that she did not have any money with her.

Getting out of Tariq's Parisian home had been, in retrospect, suspiciously easy. She had forced herself into action knowing that the alternative involved the fetal position and a very long cry, neither of which she could allow herself. So after she had taken a shower in the luxurious bathroom suite, scrubbing herself nearly raw in water almost too hot to bear, as if that would remove the feel of him from her skin, Jessa had pulled on one of the seductively comfortable robes set out by the unseen staff and tried to see if she could find something to wear. Her blue sheath dress from the night before had been a crumpled mess, and, in any case, she'd been unable to bring herself to wear it again—she couldn't bear to remember how he had removed it. How she had *wanted* him to remove it.

She'd snuck down to the lower levels of the house, looking for the guest suites that she knew must be somewhere, because how could there fail to be guest rooms in such a house? The house was, as she had only noticed in passing awe the night before, magnificent. Glorious works of art by identifiably famous artists graced the walls, a Vermeer here, a Picasso there, though Jessa had not spared them more than a glance. A sculpture she was almost positive she'd seen a copy of in a London museum occupied an entire atrium all its own.

She'd wondered where Tariq's offices were—purely because she'd wanted to avoid him, she told herself—and had frozen in place each time she'd heard a footfall or a low voice, or had eased open a new door to peer behind it. She'd finally found what she was looking for in a set of rooms hidden away in a closed-off wing on the second floor: a closet filled with women's clothes in a variety of sizes.

She'd pulled on a pair of black wool trousers that were slightly too big, and the softest charcoal-gray linen button-down blouse she had ever worn, that was a bit tighter across the chest than she would have chosen on her own. Then she'd found a pair of black-and-brown ballet-style flats, only the tiniest bit too big for her feet. A black wool jacket completed the outfit and, once she smoothed her hair into some kind of order, had made Jessa look like someone far wealthier and much calmer.

It was remarkable, she'd thought, peering into the standing mirror in the corner of the dressing room, that she could look so pulled-together on the outside when she was still too afraid to look at the raw mess on the inside.

She had felt it, though. The sob that might take her at any moment, might suck her down into the heaving mass of emotion she could feel swirling inside, ready to spill over at the slightest provocation…

But there had been no time to think about such things. She had shaken the feelings off, reminding herself that there was only Jeremy to think about, only his welfare and nothing else. She had to get out of Tariq's house, and as far away from him as possible, before she was tempted to share with him things she had never shared, not in their entirety, with anyone.

Jessa had expected it to be difficult to find her way out of the house—had expected, in fact, to be apprehended by Tariq or his staff or *someone*—and had found herself a curious mixture of disappointed and elated when she'd simply walked down the impressive marble stair and let herself out onto the elegant Paris street beyond.

It had been chillier outside than she'd expected, and wet. She hadn't made it to the first corner before it had started to rain in earnest, and the clothes she'd liberated from the closet were little help. Her mind had raced with every step she took. She couldn't go home to York, could she? It would be the obvious place for Tariq to look, and if he was as serious as she worried he must be about tearing into her life, he was much more likely to stumble upon something there than anywhere else. Jessa had walked until she hit a major boulevard, and then had looked at a map at one of the kiosks. She could hardly take in the fact that she was in Paris, one of the most celebrated cities in the world. She had been much too focused on Tariq and what he might do, and how he might do it.

While she walked, the perfect solution had come to her. Friends of hers from home had gone on a holiday last year, and had taken the train from Paris to Rome. Rome was even farther away from Jeremy. Should Tariq come after her as he'd threatened to do, she would be leading him away from his true quarry. So she'd found the train station on the map, happily located not too far away, and had walked.

She walked and walked, down streets she had only ever seen in photographs, the borrowed shoes rubbing at her cold toes and slapping the pavement beneath her feet. She walked past the soaring glory of the Arc de Triomphe and down the Champs-Elysées, the wide boulevard glistening in the rain, achingly beautiful despite the overcast skies above. She walked in and out of puddles in the Jardin des Tuileries, still crowded with tourists under bright umbrellas, toward the iconic glass pyramid that heralded the entrance to the Louvre. She took shelter from the rain in the famed arcades that stretched beneath the great buildings along the Rue de Rivoli, filled with brightly lit shops and the bustling energy of city life.

And if tears fell from her eyes and rolled down her cheeks as she walked, tears for Tariq and for herself and for all the things she'd lost, they were indistinguishable from the rain.

It was only when she'd finally made her way into the impressive rail station with the huge clock tower that reminded her of Big Ben back home in the UK that the reality of her situation had hit her.

She had no money. And, worse, no access to any money.

She'd tucked her bank card into her evening bag before she'd left her home in York last night, but she hadn't thought to bring it with her when she'd left Tariq's house. She'd been entirely too focused on getting out of there to think about such practicalities.

Once again, she was a fool.

All of the emotions that Jessa had been trying to hold at bay rushed at her then like a tidal wave, forcing her to stop walking in the middle of the crowded station. She thought her knees might give out from under her. She was nearly trampled by the relentless stream of commuters and holidaymakers on all sides as they raced through the building, headed for trains and destinations far away from here. But Jessa was trapped. Stranded. How could she possibly keep Jeremy a secret if she couldn't even take a simple train journey to somewhere, anywhere else? She was soaked through to her skin: cold, wet, miserable, and alone in Paris. She had no money, and the one person she knew in the city was the last person on earth she could go to for help.

What was she going to do?

She felt a hand on her arm and immediately turned, jostled out of the dark spiral she was in.

"Excuse me," she began, apologetically.

But it was Tariq.

He wore another dark suit, expertly fitted to showcase his lean hunter's physique, and a matching scowl. He held her elbow in his large hand much too securely. She did not have to try to jerk away from him to know she would not be able to do so if he didn't allow it. She had no doubt she looked pathetic—like a drowned rat. Meanwhile, he looked like what he was: a very powerful man at the end of his patience.

She hated the way he looked at her, as if she had done something unspeakable to him. When she had only ever acted to protect Jeremy! Hadn't she? She hated that he did not say a word, and only seared her straight through with that dark glare of his. She hated most of all that some part of her was relieved to see him, that that same traitorous part of her wanted him to rescue her, as if he was not the one responsible for her predicament in the first place!

Her eyes burned with tears. He only stared at her, his dark eyes penetrating, implacable. She felt her mouth open, but she could not speak.

What could she say? She didn't know whether to be relieved or appalled that he was beside her, even though he was what she had run from. She only knew there was an ache inside that seemed to intensify with every breath, and it had nothing at all to do with sex. It had to do with the way he looked at her, as if he was disappointed in her. As if she had wounded him in ways words could not express. She couldn't imagine why that should hurt her in return, but it did.

"Come," he said, his voice a powerful rumble yet curiously devoid of anger, which made the dampness at the back of her eyes threaten to spill over again. "The car is waiting."

The damned woman was likely to catch her death of pneumonia, Tariq thought darkly, which would not suit him at all, as she still kept so many secrets from him. As he stepped outside the station, two of his aides leaped to attention, umbrellas in hand, and sheltered them both as Tariq led her to the sleek black car that waited by the curb. Not that an umbrella would do her any good at this point. She might as well have jumped, fully dressed, into the Seine.

His driver opened the back door and Tariq handed Jessa inside, then climbed in after her, sitting so he could look at her beside him. He watched her settle into her seat and told himself he did not notice the way the soaking wet shirt clung to her curves, leaving nothing at all to the imagination. Not that he needed to imagine what he could still taste on his tongue and feel beneath his hands. He wordlessly handed her a bath towel as the car pulled into traffic.

"Thank you."

Her voice was hushed. Almost formal. She looked at the towel on her lap for a moment and then raised her head. Her eyes seemed too wide, too bright, and haunted, somehow. To his surprise, the anger that had consumed him earlier had subsided. Which was not to say he was happy with her, or had forgotten what she'd done to him—the lies she was still telling with her continued silence—but the fury that had seized him and forced him to walk away from her rather than unleash it in her presence had simmered to a low boil and then faded into something far more painful. Anger was easy, in comparison.

He didn't know why. He had been coldly furious all day, and doubly so when she'd left the house. He had had his people monitor her movements as a matter of course, and had seethed about it while he ought to have been concentrating on his official duties. When it became clear where she was headed and he had called for the car, he had felt the crack of his temper, but somehow the sight of her standing in the middle of the busy train station had gotten to him. She had looked so forlorn, so lost. Not at all the warrior woman with more fire and courage than sense who had made love to him all night long. Who had stood up to him consistently since he'd walked back into her life. By the time he'd reached her side, he had been amazed to discover that the angry words on his tongue had dissolved, unsaid.

Yet he still had the echo of what she'd said earlier ricocheting in his head, close as it was to something his uncle had said to him years before: *What kind of man are you?* The kind who terrorized women into risking pneumonia on the streets of Paris, apparently. The kind whose former lover defied him to her own detriment, throwing herself out into a cold autumn rain rather than tell him what had become of their child. What kind of man was he, indeed, to inspire these things?

He watched her towel off her face, then try to tend to the sopping mass of her hair. She shivered.

"You are cold."

"No," she said, but there was no force behind it.

"Your teeth are about to chatter," he said with little patience. Would she rather freeze to death than accept his help? *Obstinate woman.* He leaned forward to press the intercom button, then ordered the heat turned on. "See? Was that so difficult?"

She looked at him, her eyes dark and wary, then away.

"I hope you had a pleasant walk," he continued, his tone sardonic. "My men tell me you nearly drowned in a puddle outside the Louvre."

She looked startled for a moment. "Your men?"

"Of course." His brows rose. "You cannot imagine that a king's residence is left so wide open, can you? That any passerby could stroll in and out on a whim? I told you what would happen if you left."

"I didn't..." She broke off. She swallowed. "You have security. Of course you do." She shrugged slightly. "I never saw them."

Tariq leveled a look at her, lounging back against his seat, taking care not to touch her. Touching her had not led where he had expected it to lead. He had meant to control her and rid himself of this obsession, and instead had risked himself in ways he would have thought impossible. Felt things he was not prepared to examine. *Damn her.*

"If you saw them, they would not be very good at their jobs, would they?" he asked idly.

Silence fell, heavy and deep, between them. She continued to try to dry herself, and he continued to watch her attempts, but something had shifted. He didn't know what it was. Her desperate, doomed escape attempt that had proved her brave, if reckless? Or the fact that she looked not unlike a child as she sat there, as bedraggled as a kitten, her eyes wide and defeated?

"Why did you stop walking in the station?" he asked

without knowing he meant to speak. "You were nearly run down where you stood."

She let out a rueful laugh. "I have no money," she said. She met his gaze as if she expected him to comment, but he only lifted a brow in response.

"And what now?" she asked softly, that defiant tilt to her chin, though her hair was still dark and wet against her face, making her seem pale and small. "Am I your prisoner?"

There was a part of him that wanted to rage at her still. But he had not forgotten, even in his fury, even now, how she had somehow touched him once again, gotten under his skin. He, who had believed himself inviolate in that way. How he had yearned for her all of these years, though he had made up any number of lies to excuse it. How he had waited for her to wake this morning, loath to disturb her. He suspected that a great deal of his anger stemmed from that knowledge, that even as she defied him and lied to him, insulted him and dared him to do his worst, he admired her for it. It had taken him hours, and perhaps the sight of her dogged determination to get away from him in order to keep her secrets no matter what the cost to herself, to understand that truth, however uncomfortable it made him.

What kind of man are you?

And could he truly blame her for what she'd done, whatever she'd done? asked a ruthless inner voice. Given what she knew of him back then—a liar, a wastrel—why would she want to share a child with him? It was as his uncle had told him. He had not been a man. He had had nothing to offer any child.

"I need to know what happened," he said quietly. He did not look at her, watching instead the blurred Parisian buildings and monuments as they sped past.

"So the answer is yes. I am your prisoner." She let out a breath. "For how long?"

He could have said, for as long as he liked. He could have reminded her that he was a king, that he could have absolute power over her if he wished it. Instead, he turned to her and met her troubled gaze.

"Until you tell me what I want to know," he said.

"Forever, then," she said, her voice hollow. "You plan to hold me against my will forever."

"When have you been held against your will?" he asked, though his voice held no heat. "I do not recall your demands to leave last night. And I did not prevent you from leaving this morning."

"With no money," she said bitterly. "Where was I supposed to go?"

"If you are without funds, Jessa," he replied evenly, "you need only ask."

"I have my own money, thank you," she said at once, sharply.

"Then why didn't you use it?" he asked. She sighed and dropped her gaze to her hands. Again, silence stretched between them, seeming to implicate them both.

"Isn't this where you threaten me some more?" she asked softly, her attention directed at her lap. Yet somehow her voice seemed to tug at him. To shame him. "That you'll tear apart my whole life, make it a living hell?"

What kind of man are you?

Tariq expelled a long breath and rubbed at his temples with his fingers. When he spoke, he hardly recognized his own voice.

"You must understand that when I say I am the last of my bloodline, I am not only talking about lines of succession and historical footnotes that will be recorded when I am gone," he said, not knowing what he meant to say. Not recognizing the gruffness in his own voice. "I was orphaned when I was still a child, Jessa. I was not yet three. I don't know if the little I remember of my parents is real or if I have internalized photographs and stories told to me by others."

"Tariq." She said his name on a sigh, almost as if she hurt for him.

"My uncle's family was the only family I ever knew," he said, with an urgency he didn't entirely understand. She bit her lower lip and worried it between her teeth. "I thought I was the only one left. Until today."

"I don't know what you want me to say," she whispered, her voice thick.

"Do I have a child?" he asked her, appalled at the uncertainty he could hear in his own voice. He didn't know what he would do if she threw it back at him as he knew she could. "Is my family more than simply me?"

Her eyes squeezed shut, and she made a sound that was much like a sob, though she covered her mouth with her hand. For a long moment they sat in silence, the only sound the watery swish of traffic outside the car, and her ragged breathing. He thought she would not answer. He felt a new bleakness settle upon him. Would he never know what had happened? Would he be condemned to wonder? Was it no more than he deserved for the way he had behaved in his former life, the way he had treated her, the way he had treated himself and his family, his many squandered gifts?

But she turned her head to look at him, her cinnamon eyes bright with a pain he didn't fully understand.

"I don't know that I can make you feel any better about this," she said, her voice thick and rough. "But I will tell you what I know."

CHAPTER TWELVE

JESSA didn't know why she had said anything, why his obvious pain had moved her so much that she broke her silence so suddenly. She hadn't meant to say a word. And then she'd heard the raw agony in his voice and something inside had snapped. Or loosened. She had thought she might cry. Instead, she had spoken words she'd never meant to speak aloud and certainly not to him.

But the truth was, he hadn't meant to leave her, had he? His uncle had died—his whole family had died. What was he supposed to have done? It had occurred to her, somewhere out in all the cold and wet of the Paris streets, that somewhere along the line it had become important for her to keep blaming him for leaving her because it kept the attention away from what had happened after he left. From the decisions she had made that he had had no part in. Was that what she had been hiding from?

Tariq said nothing. He only looked at her for a long moment, his gaze fathomless, and then nodded once. Definitively. She expected him to demand she tell him everything she could at once, but instead he remained silent for the rest of their short journey to his grand house. Once there, he ushered her back to the suite of rooms on the top floor that she had run from earlier. Was it to be her prison? Jessa felt too raw, too exposed, to give that question the thought she knew she should.

No sign of their long, passionate night remained in the exquisite room. The great bed was returned to its ivory-and-gold splendor, and warm lights glowed from sconces in the wall, setting off the fine moldings and Impressionist art that graced the walls. Jessa stood in the center of the room, deliberately not looking at the bed, deliberately not remembering, and swallowed. Hard.

"You will wish to clean up, I think," Tariq said, an odd politeness in his tone as if they did not know each other. And yet, he anticipated her needs. He gestured toward the spacious dressing room that was adjacent to the palatial bathroom. "I have taken the liberty of having clothes laid out for you that will, I hope, fit."

Jessa looked down at the sodden mess of the clothes she wore, and swallowed again, not sure she could speak. She didn't know how to process his thoughtfulness. Perhaps he was simply tired of looking at her in such a bedraggled state. She was tired of it herself—her shoes so soaked that she could hear her toes squelch into them each time she moved. The room, for all it was large and elegant beyond imagining, seemed too close, too hushed around them. She was afraid to meet his gaze. Afraid she had opened herself up too far, and he would see too much.

Afraid that once she bared herself to him again, he would break her heart as surely and as completely as he had done before.

"There are matters that require my attention," he said after a long moment, still in that stiff way. As if he was as nervous as she was. "I cannot put them off."

"I understand," she managed to say, frowning fiercely at her wet, cold shoes.

"I will return as soon as I can." He sighed slightly and she risked looking at him. "You will wait here?"

Not run away, he meant. Not continue to keep her secrets. Stay and tell him what she'd said she would.

Share with him what should never have been a secret, what should have been theirs. Together.

"I will." It was like a vow.

They stared at each other for a long, fraught moment. Jessa could feel her pulse beat in her ears, her throat.

He nodded to her, so stiff and formal it was like a bow, and strode from the room.

It was already evening when a diffident maid in a pressed black uniform led Jessa through the maze of the house to find Tariq. He waited for her in a cozy, richly appointed room that featured a crackling fire in a stone fireplace, walls of books and deep leather couches. Tariq stood with his back to the door, his stance wide and his hands clasped behind him, staring out the French doors at the wet blue dusk beyond.

Jessa stood in the doorway for a moment, filled with a confusing mix of panic, uncertainty and something else she did not wish to examine—something that felt like a hollow space in her chest as she looked at him, his face remote in profile, his strong back stiff, as if he expected nothing from her but further pain. She shook the thought away, suddenly deeply afraid in a way she had not been before—a way that had nothing to do with Jeremy and everything to do with her traitorous, susceptible heart. She smoothed her palms along the fine wool of the trousers she wore, pretending she was concerned about wrinkles when she knew, deep down, that was not true. And that it was far too late to worry.

Tariq had been as good as his word. When Jessa emerged from her second hot shower of the day, she had found an entire wardrobe laid out for her in the dressing room, complete with more grooming products than she had at her own home in York. All of it, from the clothes to the hair bands and perfumes, had been specifically chosen with her tastes in mind. It was as if Tariq knew her better than she knew herself, a line of thought she preferred not to examine more closely. Not knowing what the night held, and not wanting to send the wrong message or make herself more vulnerable than she felt already, Jessa had dressed for this conversation in tailored chocolate wool trousers and a simple white silk blouse. Over that, she'd wrapped a sky-blue cashmere concoction that was softer than anything she had ever touched before. Now she tightened the wrap around her middle, as if it alone could hold her together. She'd even smoothed her heavy mass of hair back into a high ponytail, hoping it might broadcast a certain calm strength her curls would not.

"I trust everything fits well," Tariq said in a low voice, still staring out through the French doors. Jessa started slightly, not realizing he'd known she was there.

"Perfectly," she said, and then coughed to clear the thickness from her throat.

He turned then, and Jessa was lost suddenly in the bleakness she saw on his face. It made his harsh features seem even more unapproachable and distant. She wanted to go to him, to soothe it away somehow, and then wondered who she'd confused him for, who she thought she was facing. This was still Tariq bin Khaled Al-Nur. He was more dangerous to her now, she thought, than he had ever been before. She would be wise to remember that. Oh, it was not as if she had anything to fear from him—it was her own heart she feared. Perhaps it had always been her own surrender she feared more than anything else.

"Tell me," Tariq said, and she did not mistake his meaning.

She took a deep breath. Stalling for time, she crossed the room and perched on the edge of the buttery-soft leather sofa, but did not allow herself to relax back into it. She could not look at him, so she looked instead into the fire, into the relative safety of the dancing, shimmering flames.

There would be no going back from this conversation. She was honest with herself about that, at least.

"It was a boy," she said, her head spinning, because she could not believe she was telling him this after so long. A sense of unreality gripped her as if she was dreaming all of it—the luxurious clothes, the fire, the impossibly forbidding man who stood close and yet worlds away. "I called him Jeremy."

She could feel Tariq's eyes on her then, though she dared not look at him to see what expression he wore as he digested this news. That he was, biologically, a father. Swallowing carefully, she put her hands into her lap, stared fixedly into the fire and continued.

"I found out I was pregnant when I went to the doctor's that day." She sighed, summoning up those dark days in her memory. "You had been so careful never to mention the future, never to hint—" But she couldn't blame him, not entirely. "I didn't know if it meant I would lose you, or if you would be happy. I didn't know if I was happy!" She shook her head and frowned at the flames dancing before her, heedless of the emotional turmoil just outside the stone fireplace. "That was where I went. I stopped at a friend's flat in Brighton. I...tried to work out what to do."

"Those days you went missing," Tariq said in a quiet

voice. Jessa couldn't look at him. "You hadn't left, then, after all."

"It's so ironic that you thought so," Jessa said with a hollow laugh. "As that was my biggest fear at first—that you would leave. Once you knew." She laughed again in the same flat way. "Only when I returned to London, you had already gone. And when I saw who you really were and what you had to do, I knew that you were never coming back."

Jessa took a deep breath, feeling it saw into her lungs. It would get no easier if she put it off, she thought. It might never get easier at all. She blew the breath out and forced herself to continue.

"I was such a mess," she said. "I was sacked in short order, of course. I tried to get another job in the city, not realizing that I'd been effectively blackballed. My sister wanted me to move back home to York, but that seemed such an admission of failure. I…I so wanted everything to simply go on as if nothing had ever happened. As if *you* had never happened."

She heard a faint sound like an exhalation or a muttered curse, but she couldn't look at him. She couldn't bear to see what he thought of her. She was too afraid she would never tell the story if she didn't tell him now. From the corner of her eye, she saw him move and begin to prowl around the room as if he could not bear to stand still.

"But I was pregnant, and…" How to tell him what that had felt like? The terror mixed in equal part with fierce, incomparable joy? Her hand crept over her abdomen as if she could remember by touch. As if the memory of Jeremy still kicked there, so insistent and demanding.

"You must have been quite upset," Tariq said quietly. Too quietly. Jessa stared down at her lap, threading her hands together.

"At you, perhaps. Or the situation," she said softly. "But not at the baby. I realized quickly that I wanted the baby, no matter what." She sucked in a breath. "And so I had him. He was perfect."

Her emotions were too close to the surface. Too raw, still. Or perhaps it was because she was finally sharing the story with Tariq, who should have been there five years ago. She had almost felt as if he was there in the delivery room. She had sobbed as much for the man who was not her partner and was not with her as she had for the pain she was in as each contraction twisted and ripped through her. Now she pressed her lips together to keep herself from sobbing anew, and breathed through her nose until she was sure she wouldn't cry. This was about the facts. She could give him the facts.

"I had a hard labor," she said. "There were…some complications. I was depressed, scared." She had had postpartum depression on top of her physical ailments, of course, but it had not seemed, at the time, like something she could ever come out of whole. She snuck a look at him then. He had found his way to the couch opposite, but he did not look at her as he sat there, sprawled out before the fire. He aimed his deep frown toward the dark red Persian carpet at his feet.

Jessa wondered what he was thinking. Did this seem unreal to him? Impossible? That they could be sitting in a Parisian room, so many miles and years away from the heartache that they had caused together? It boggled the mind. It made her feel dizzy.

"I had no job, and no idea where I might go to get one," Jessa continued, ignoring the thickness in her voice, the twist in her belly. "I had this perfect baby boy, the son of a king, and I couldn't give him the life that he needed. That he deserved." Her voice cracked, and she sighed, then cleared her throat. "I thought at first that it was just hormonal—just first-time mother fears, but as time went on, the feeling grew stronger."

"Why?" Tariq's voice was barely a whisper, and still so full of anguish. "What was missing in the life you gave him?"

Me, Jessa thought. *You.* But she said neither.

"I was…not myself," she said instead. "I cried all the time. I was so lost." It had been more than she could handle. The baby's constant demands. The lack of sleep. The lack of help, even though her sister had tried. Had she not been so terribly, terribly depressed—near suicidal, perhaps… But she had been. There was no point in wishing. "And how could I be a good parent? The single decision I'd made that led to my being a parent in the first place had been…" Her voice trailed off, and her gaze flew to his.

"To get pregnant accidentally," he finished for her, so matter-of-factly, so coldly. "With my child."

"Yes." Something shimmered between them, a kind of bond, though it was fragile and painful. Jessa forged on, determined to get the rest out at last. "And I had had all this time to read about you in the news, to watch you on the television, to really and truly see that nothing you had ever told me was true. That I'd made up our relationship in my head. That I was a silly girl with foolish dreams, not fit to be someone's *parent*."

He raked his hands through his hair, his expression unreadable. But he did not look away.

"Meanwhile," she continued, her voice barely a thread of sound, "there were people with intact families already. People who had done everything right, made all the right choices, and just couldn't have a baby. Why should Jeremy suffer just because his mother was a mess? How was that fair to him?"

"You gave him up for adoption," Tariq said, sounding almost dazed. "You gave him away to strangers?"

"He deserved to have everything," Jessa said fiercely, hating the emphasis he put on *strangers*—and not wanting to correct him. "Love, two adoring parents, a family. A real chance at a good life! Not…a devastated single mother who could barely take care of herself, much less him."

Tariq did not speak, though Jessa could hear his ragged breathing and see the turmoil in his expression.

"I wanted him to be happy more than I wanted him to be happy with me," she whispered.

"I thought…" Tariq stopped and rubbed his hands over his face. "I believed it was customary in an adoption to seek the permission of both parents."

Jessa bit her lower lip and braced herself. "Jeremy has only one birth parent listed on his birth certificate," she said quietly. "Me."

Tariq simply looked at her, a deep anger that verged on a grief she recognized evident in the dark depths of his troubled gaze. Jessa raised her shoulders and then let them drop. Why should she feel guilty now? And yet she did. Because neither of them had had all the choices they should have had. Neither one of them was blameless.

"I saw no reason to claim a relationship to a king for a baby when I could not claim one myself," she said.

Tariq's gaze seemed to burn, but Jessa did not look away.

"I can almost understand why you did not inform me that you were pregnant," he said after a long, tense moment. "Or I can try to understand this. But to give the child away? To give him to someone else without even allowing me to know that he existed in the first—"

"I tried to find you," she cut in, her voice thick with

emotion. "I went to the firm and begged them to contact you. I had no way to locate you!"

"No way to locate me?" He shook his head. Temper cracked like lightning in his eyes, his voice. "I am not exactly in hiding!"

"You have no idea, do you?" she asked, closing her eyes briefly. "I cannot even imagine how many young, single women must throw themselves at you. How many must tell tales to members of your staff, or your government officials, in a desperate bid for your attention. Why should I be treated any differently?" She shifted in her seat, wanting nothing more than to get up and run, end this uncomfortable conversation. Hadn't she been running from it for ages? "It's not possible to simply look you up in the phone book and give you a ring, Tariq. You must know that."

His expression told her that he didn't wish to know it. He swallowed, and she didn't know how to feel about the fact he was clearly as uncomfortable as she was. As emotional.

"I went to the firm," she said again, remembering that day some months after Jeremy had been born, when she'd been desperate and on the brink of making her decision but wanted to reach Tariq first, if she could. "They laughed at me."

It had been worse than the day they'd sacked her. The speculation in their eyes, the disdain—they had looked at her like she was dirt. Like she was worse than dirt.

"They laughed at you?" As if he didn't understand.

"Of course." She found the courage to meet his eyes. "To them I was nothing more than the slutty intern, still gold digging. One of them offered to take me out to dinner—*wink wink*."

"Wink—?" Tariq began, frowning, and then comprehension dawned and his expression turned glacial.

"Yes," Jessa confirmed. "He was happy to see if he

could sample the goods. After all, I'd been good enough for a king, for a while. But he certainly wasn't going to help me contact you."

"Who?" Tariq asked, his voice like thunder. "Who was the man?"

"It doesn't really matter, does it? I doubt very much he was the only one who thought that way." Jessa shook her head and looked back into the fire, sinking further into the embrace of the cashmere over her shoulders. "I realized that I would have to make the decision on my own. That there was absolutely no way I could talk to you about it. We might as well have never met."

"So you did it." There was no question in his voice. Only that scratchiness and a heavy kind of resignation.

"When he was four months old," Jessa said, surprised to feel herself get choked up. "I kissed him goodbye and I gave him what he could never have if I kept him." She closed her eyes against the pain that never really left her, no matter what she did or what she told herself. "And now he has everything any child could hope for. Two parents who dote on him, who treat him like a miracle—not a mistake. Not something unplanned that had to be dealt with." She could feel the wetness on her cheeks but made no move to wipe it away.

"You don't regret this decision?" His voice seemed to come from far away. Jessa turned to look at him, her heart so raw she thought it might burst from within.

"I regret it *every day*!" she whispered at him fiercely. Unequivocally. "I miss him *every moment*!"

Tariq sat forward, his eyes intent on hers. "Then I do not see why we cannot—"

"He is *happy*!" she interrupted him, emotion making her forceful. But he had to hear her. "He is happy, Tariq.

Content. I know that I did the right thing for him, and that's the only thing that matters. Not what I feel. And not what you feel, either, no matter if you are a king or not. He is a happy, healthy little boy with two parents who are not us." Her voice trembled then, and the tears spilled over and trailed across her cheeks. "Who will never be us."

She buried her face in her hands, not entirely sure why she was crying like this—as desperately as if it had just happened, as if she had just accepted that it was real. It had to do with telling Tariq the truth finally. Or most of the truth, in any case—all the most important parts of the truth. It was as if some part of her she'd scarcely known existed had held on to the fantasy that as long as he did not know, it could not have happened. It could not be true. And now she had lost even that lie to tell herself.

Jessa did not know how long she wept, but she knew when he came to sit beside her, his much heavier body next to hers on the leather making her sag toward him. He did not whisper false words of encouragement. He did not rant or rave or rail against her. He did not plot ways to change this harsh reality, or ask questions she could not answer.

He merely put his arm around her, guided her head to his shoulder and let her cry.

It was late when Tariq got off the phone with his attorneys, having confirmed what he'd suspected but still didn't quite want to accept: British adoptions were relatively rare, and well-nigh irreversible. When the child came of age, he could seek out his parents through a national register if he chose, but not before. And British courts were notoriously unsympathetic to anyone who tried to reverse the adoption process—claiming they acted in the best interests of the child and sought to cause as little disruption as possible.

He left his office and made his way back to the small library where he'd left Jessa when she'd finally succumbed to the stress and emotion of the day and had drifted off to sleep. He found her curled up on the leather sofa, her hands beneath her cheek, looking more like a child than a woman who could have borne one. Much less borne his.

Some part of him still wanted to unleash the temper that rolled and burned inside of him on her, to hurt her because he hurt, but he found he could not. He looked at her and felt only a deep sadness and a growing possessiveness that he wasn't sure he understood. He knew he wanted to blame her because it would be convenient, nothing more.

The truth was that he blamed himself. He was everything his uncle had accused him of being, and while he had known that enough so that he'd altered his life to honor his uncle's passing, he had not understood the true scope of it until now.

He might have spent years haunted by her, but he had not wanted to deal with the young woman who had made his dissipated heart ask questions he hadn't wanted to answer, and so he had excised her when he left England just as he had excised everything that reminded him of his old life. He had transformed himself into the man his uncle wanted him to be, and he'd done it brutally. What would it have cost him to seek her out after the accident, even for something as little as a phone call? What kind of man left a young, obviously infatuated girl in the lurch like that? Had he allowed himself to think about it for even a moment, he would have known that she'd have been devastated first by his disappearance, and then by the shocking truth about who he was. How could he now turn around and blame her for making what she'd thought were the best decisions she could under those circumstances?

After all, she had not known how deeply she had touched him then, and how she had continued to prey on his thoughts for all of those years. Only he had known it, and he had barely allowed the truth of his feelings for her to register. He had buried them with his uncle, buried them with all the remnants of his former life, buried them all and told himself that he preferred his life that way. That Jessa herself was tainted by her association with his former, profligate self, and thus could never be considered a possible consort or queen for the King of Nur. The kind of woman who would fall in love with Tariq the black sheep was by definition unfit for the king. And if he woke in the night and heard her voice, or felt phantom fingers trail along his skin, no one had ever needed to know that but him.

And yet he had still gone to find her, breaking all of his own rules, telling himself any number of lies—anything to be near her once again. Had he known even then that one night could never be enough? Had that been why he had fought against it for so long?

He stooped to shift her from the couch into his arms, lifting her high against his chest and carrying her with him through the house, aware that something in him whispered that she belonged there, that she fit there perfectly. She nestled against him, her body easy with him in sleep in a way she would never be were she awake. He felt a sudden pang of nostalgia for the freely given love of the young girl he'd so callously thrown away. She felt good so close against him. She felt like his.

In his rooms, he deposited her gently on the bed, removing her shoes and pulling the coverlet over her. For a moment he gazed down at her, watching her breathe, and let the strange tenderness he felt wash through him. He did not try to judge it, or deny it. He thought of what it must have been like for her, to be so alone, abandoned and forced into so difficult a position. They were not that different, the two of them, he thought. Each of them thrust, alone, into positions they had never meant to occupy.

Without letting himself think it through, he climbed into the bed behind her, pulling her close, so her back was flush against his chest, her bottom nestled between his thighs. He inhaled deeply, letting her distinct scents wash over him, soothing him, letting him imagine that they could both heal. Jasmine in her hair, and something sweet and warm beneath that he knew was simply Jessa. Vanilla and heat.

She stirred, and he knew when she woke by the sudden tension in her body where before there was only languor. He smoothed a hand down her side, tracing the curves of her body, as if he could erase what she had suffered so easily.

"I did not mean to fall asleep," she whispered into the dark room. She moved under his hands, as if testing her boundaries, as if she thought she was his prisoner.

Tariq did not respond. He only held her and pretended he did not know why he could not let her go.

"In the morning," she continued, her voice much too careful, much too polite, "I will head home. I think it's best." She moved as if to separate from him, and he let his arm fall away from her when he wanted only to hold on, to keep her close, as if she was sunlight and he was an acre of frozen earth, desperate for winter to end.

"Tariq?" She turned toward him. He twisted over onto his back, aware of a different kind of need surging through him. A need for peace, the peace that only holding her close had ever brought him. "Should I find somewhere else to sleep?" she asked, her voice tentative. Scared. Of him. And why shouldn't she be, after the things he had done?

He could not bear it. And he refused to think about why.

And then, from that place inside him that he could not fully admit existed, yet could no longer ignore, he whispered, "I do not want you to go, Jessa. Not yet."

CHAPTER THIRTEEN

ONE week passed, and then another, and the subject of Jessa's departure did not come up again. Jessa had made the necessary calls home to her sister and to her boss, and had taken the long overdue vacation time she was owed that she had never bothered to take before.

"*Where* are you?" her sister Sharon had asked, shocked, when Jessa got her on the phone. "Since when do you run off on a holiday at the drop of a hat?"

"I had an urge to see Paris, that's all," Jessa had lied.

"I wish I could swan off to Paris on a lark!" Sharon had said. And then the time to mention who she was with and why she was with him had passed the moment Sharon put down the phone, so it had remained Jessa's secret.

It wasn't that she was trying to hide the fact that she was with Tariq from her sister, necessarily, but she wasn't planning to trumpet it from the rooftops, either. She told herself that there was nothing unusual in it; she and Tariq were simply giving themselves some space and time to process the loss of Jeremy together rather than apart. Who else could understand how it felt? They were being healthy, she thought, modern; and part of her believed it.

Jessa had all of Paris to explore each day, as Tariq spent

his time closeted in meetings or on the telephone with his advisors, political allies, and business contacts—tending to his kingdom from afar.

"Tell me what you saw today," Tariq asked each evening, and Jessa would relate stories of freshly baked baguettes, lazy afternoons in cafés, or walking tours of famous monuments. Each evening she tried harder to make him smile. Each evening she found herself more and more invested in whether or not she succeeded.

"I have always loved Paris," Tariq told her one night as they lingered over coffee out in one of the city's famous restaurants, where the service was so impeccable that Jessa almost felt compelled to apologize every time she shifted in her chair. "My uncle used this residence as a vacation home, but I prefer to use it as a base for my European business concerns." He leaned back against his chair in an indolent way that called attention to all the power he kept caged in his lean, muscled frame.

"What isn't to love?" Jessa agreed with a happy smile, propping her elbow on the table and resting her chin on her hand. She could look at him for hours. His face alone compelled her—all that harshness and cruelty tempered by the keen intelligence in his eyes. "It mixes magic with practicality."

It was as if she had forgotten they had ever felt like adversaries, though, of course, she had not. This sweet truce between them was far more dangerous than the wars they had already fought and survived. She was so much more at risk when he looked at her the way he did tonight, with something she so desperately wanted to call tenderness.

"Indeed," he agreed now, and their eyes caught, something more potent than the rich brew in their cups surging between them, making Jessa's pulse race.

"Tariq," she said softly, not wishing to break the spell between them but knowing she should speak, knowing she should acknowledge the truth of things, "you know that I—"

"Come," he said, pushing back from the table. "We shall walk home along the Seine and you will tell me which Van Gogh in the Musée d'Orsay you prefer."

"I cannot possibly choose," she said, but she let him pull her to her feet, exulting in the slide of his palm against hers. *Why not dream a little longer?* she asked herself. Who would it hurt?

"Then you must tell me about the Musée Rodin instead," he said, taking a moment too long before releasing her hand and stepping back to pull out her chair. "I have not been in many years."

Jessa had studied every luscious, supple curve of stone in the museum he mentioned, and had marveled at the raw sensual power of marble statues that should have seemed cold and dead yet instead begged to be touched, caressed. As she thought she might do at any moment.

But Tariq only took her arm and ushered her out into the soft Parisian night.

Sharing Jeremy's adoption with him had changed something, Jessa realized as they walked together along the banks of the Seine in a silence that was not quite comfortable—too charged was it with their simmering chemistry and the restraint they had shown in not touching each other in so long. Not since that first night.

Later, back at the grand house, when Tariq had politely excused himself and she was left in the lonely expanse of the bedroom suite, she thought more about the evening's revelation. Jeremy was not her private pain now, to hoard and to hurt herself with. It was theirs to share, and the sharing not only lessened the hurt, it removed all the walls she'd built around it. In place of those walls was something far too delicate and shimmering to name. She did not want to think about when she had felt this way before, and what had become of her.

"You are such a fool," she whispered aloud, her voice swallowed up by the ornate furnishings all around her.

But she also did not want to think about the one crucial bit of information she had withheld from him. The one small yet crucial fact about Jeremy she had not been able to bring herself to share. She could not quite trust him with it, could she? Not when she knew deep down that this was a fantasy she was living in, something that would not, *could not* last. Protecting Jeremy was forever. It had to be.

It was as if, Jessa thought as she changed her clothes for dinner a few nights later, having hurt each other so terribly and so irrevocably they were now both easing their way into enjoying each other's company, as if that might make the pain lessen. As if it could make it bearable somehow.

She twisted her hair into a chignon, gathering her heavy copper curls at the nape of her neck and pinning them into place, then looked at herself in the mirror of the dressing room. She felt like Cinderella. With her hair up in the casually elegant bun, she thought she looked a bit like Cinderella, too. It was so easy to get used to the life she'd been living these past weeks, without a care in the world, wandering Paris by day and exploring the many facets of Tariq's beguiling mind at night. The dressing room contained an array of clothes tailored to her precise measurements, all of which fit perfectly and made her look like someone other than Jessa Heath of Fulford: office manager in a letting agency and all-around nobody.

The Jessa she saw in the mirror was no ordinary Yorkshire lass. Tariq had mentioned the evening would be formal, and so she wore a floor-length satin gown the color of buttercream. It whispered and murmured seductively as she moved, the neckline plunging to hint at her breasts and the perfumed hollow between, then catching her at the waist before falling in lush folds to the ground. Her back was very nearly bare, with only thin angled shoulder straps to hold the gown in place. Though Jessa would have thought her very English paleness would look sickly in a gown so light, the color instead seemed to make her skin glow. Her freckles seemed like bursts of vibrant color rather than an embarrassment.

"You are lovely," a familiar voice said from behind her, causing Jessa to start, though of course she knew who she would see when she looked in the mirror. Her body knew without having to hear the words he spoke. It reacted to the very sound of his voice, the hint of his nearness, with the now familiar rush of wild heat that suffused her.

Tariq stood in the entry to the dressing room, mouthwateringly debonair in his tuxedo, his long, strong body packaged to breathtaking perfection. His eyes seemed more green than usual, standing out from his dark hair and the black suit like some kind of deep forest beacon. His hard features seemed more handsome than fierce tonight, more approachable. Jessa felt a little stunned herself.

"Am I late?" she asked, feeling unaccountably shy suddenly in the face of so much steely male beauty. It was unfair that any one man could exude as much raw magnetism as he did, and so carelessly. She met his gaze in the mirror and then looked away, heat staining in her cheeks.

"Not at all," he said, and she knew he lied. There was a certain tenderness in his eyes that she could not account for, and could not seem to handle—it made it hard to breathe.

"Where are we going?" she asked.

The room around them seemed to contract and she pretended she was unaffected, that her nipples did not tighten to rigid points, that she could not feel the pull low in her belly. Sometimes he put his hand in the small of her back to guide her, or helped her out of a car, and though she felt even his smallest touch in every part of her being, that had been the extent of it. Though they had spent their first night together in every conceivable position, a vivid and carnal exploration of their passion, they had spent the weeks since merely talking—a curious inversion that was starting to make her shaky with need. He did not sleep with her at night and yet she knew with a deep, feminine certainty that he wanted her as much, if not more, than before.

"I must attend a benefit dinner," Tariq said, and shrugged. "It is of little importance. A dinner, a speech or two, and some dancing. You will be bored beyond reason."

As if that were possible when she was with this man. Jessa forced a smile, determined not to let the deeper emotions she could feel boiling within her spill over. This was a dream, nothing more. Cinderella went to the ball, and she would too, but that was all there was to it. The rest of the story did not apply, had never applied. She had no right to dream any Cinderella dreams, and she knew it.

"I am ready," she said, turning to him, and then stopped, caught by the arrested look on his face. As if he had been waiting for those words, but in a different context. Something unnamed but no less heavy crowded the room, narrowing the distance between them, making her pulse pound.

"Tariq?" Her voice was barely a whisper of sound.

He stood for a moment, his gaze consuming her, his mouth a flat, hard line that against all reason she longed to press her own lips against. Her heart kicked in her chest.

For a moment it seemed as if he might close the distance between them. His eyes dropped to caress her mouth, and Jessa felt it as surely as if he'd used his fingers. Her lips parted slightly, yearning for him.

"Very well then," he said, his voice rough, in his eyes all the things he had not done, all the ways he had not touched her. "Let us go."

Tariq bin Khaled Al-Nur's version of a party of no importance, Jessa found, was in fact a star-studded gala of epic proportions. Dignitaries, politicians and European nobles brushed elbows with cinema stars and international celebrities, in a shower of flashbulbs that overtook one of the famous arcades. The gala took place in a sumptuous hotel near the Place Vendôme and the Jardin des Tuileries, which Tariq confided had less historical significance than the hotel liked to admit. Jessa hardly knew where to look—from the frescoes adorning the ceiling of the reception room to the colossal gilt chandeliers that hung overhead to the rich red of the thick drapes and carpets. She felt as if she were in another world. A dream within a dream.

But this world was one in which Tariq was a king, and treated as such—not merely Tariq, her former lover. Jessa had known he was a powerful man, but she had never seen him in his element before except on television. Tonight, the fact that Tariq was an imperial power was made clear to her in a thousand little ways. It was the near-fawning deference he was shown, the deep bows he was accorded. It was the visible respect of the aides who ran interference for him, tending to his every wish and deflecting those whom he did not wish to interact with. It was the way everyone called him *Your Highness* or

Excellency, when they dared address him at all. Men Jessa only recognized from the news pulled him aside to whisper in his ear.

Once again, Jessa had the odd sensation that the world was shifting beneath her feet. It was one thing to know that Tariq was a king. What did that mean, in the abstract, shut up together in rooms where first and foremost she saw him as a man? It was something else again to really witness what it was for him to be a king, and, she could not help but think, that this was how he was treated in a country not his own. What must it be like when he was at home in Nur? Even among his peers, Tariq stood apart. He was harder, tougher. He was a warrior among bureaucrats.

She had no right to the fantasies that crept in, teasing her when she was less than vigilant. She knew her place in the world. Tariq was meant for a queen, not Jessa. Never Jessa.

"You seem unusually quiet," he said into her ear at one point, as they waited for dinner to be served. She could feel his breath fanning along her skin, teasing her nerve endings. She held back a shiver of delight.

"I am merely basking in Your Excellency's shadow," she replied, smiling at him. His hard mouth kicked up in the corner, surprising her. She snuck a look around the table. Here sat a recognizable head of state, there lounged an internationally acclaimed philanthropist; everyone exuded power of one kind or another.

"I imagine it must go to your head," she said.

He did not pretend to misunderstand her. "It is who I have become," he said simply, his gaze direct. Proud.

Had part of her been resistant to the very idea of his elevation in rank and status, even from a distance? Had she hoped, somewhere deep inside, that the doctor's son she'd loved so totally was the real Tariq and the wildly powerful king only a bad dream? Back then, he had simply been a man, however complicated. And now he was a king, and even more complicated. It was not only his job, his role. It was how he saw the world. It was who he was, every cell and every breath.

"Yes," she said softly. "I see that." She longed to touch him, but she did not dare. She did not know if there were rules of etiquette to follow, boundaries to observe.

"I cannot change the past," he said, and suddenly it was as if no one existed save the two of them. She forgot about rules, or other eyes, and drank him in.

"Neither can I," she replied without looking away.

So much loss. So many years wasted, a whole life created and given away to others. But could she honestly say she would change any part of it? Knowing that it resulted in a happy, thriving Jeremy? Something sharp twisted through her then, reminding her that she had not told him everything—could not tell him everything, even now.

"Perhaps it is time we stop looking back, then, you and I," Tariq said in a hushed voice, no less powerful for its low volume. It made something inside swell with a quiet kind of wonder, pushing all else aside.

"Where should we look?" She was in awe of what loomed between them, that made her fingers tremble and her eyes bright with a wild heat, though she refused to name it. She refused.

Tariq lifted her hand to his mouth and placed a kiss on the back of it, never breaking eye contact, not even when he sucked gently on the knuckle and made her gasp. Heat seared through her, melting her. The fire was never gone when he was near—it was only ever banked. Waiting for a trigger, a spark.

"I am sure we'll think of something," he said huskily.

* * *

Tariq turned to her the moment they crossed the threshold into the house, sweeping her into his arms and fastening his mouth to hers. He could not get enough of her taste, her heat, the soft and warm feel of her pressed against him. Jessa melted against him, her softness inflaming him, looping her arms around the column of his neck and arching into him. He tasted her again and again, exploring her mouth, feeling the kick of her immediate, uninhibited response flood through him.

Once again, he lifted her into his arms and carried her toward the bedroom, up the great stairs and toward their rooms on the top floor. Her fingers toyed with the ends of his hair where it brushed the top of his collar. Her eyes gleamed in the low lights of the quiet house around them while a secret, feminine smile curved her lips.

There were so many things he wanted to say, but he did not know where to start. He only knew that she had become necessary to him. Their tangled history was wrapped around him and growing tighter by the day, making it hard to breathe when she was not within reach. He found his way into the bedroom and set her down, unable to look away. One breath. Another.

She made a soft noise and reached out for him, her small hands framing his face, and pulled his mouth to hers. She tasted like honey and wine and went straight to his head, his heart, his aching hardness.

He set her away from him, turning her so he could look at the expanse of her creamy skin bared by the open back of her gown. He put his mouth, open and hot, on the tender nape of her neck, just to make her moan. He traced her spine with his fingers, making her shiver.

"All night I have wondered how soft your skin would be when I touched it," he told her in a low murmur, continuing to taste and touch. "You are better than crème brûlée, sweet and rich."

She let out a laugh, and the small sound ignited something in him, wild and hot and out of control.

He walked her over to the high bed, bending her forward until she braced herself on her elbows against the mattress. He heard the soft exclamation that she blew out on a sigh, or perhaps her breathing was as ragged as his. She turned her head, peering over her shoulder at him, her cinnamon eyes wide and inviting. Her lips parted, and he was certain he could hear the beat of her heart under his own skin. He held her gaze as he slowly pulled her gown up over her trim ankles, her shapely calves, her knees—

"Tariq, please…" It was a moan.

He knelt down between her open thighs, pushing the soft folds of material out of his way, marveling that her skin was softer than the satin of her gown. He pressed a kiss to the hollow behind her knee, the curve of her thigh, the crease where her thigh ended and her lush round bottom began. He curled his fingers into the soft scrap of material that covered her sex, and pulled her panties down and out of his way, helping her step out of them before he tossed them aside. He could feel her tremble. He ran his hands up her legs, testing her flesh beneath his palms. He leaned in close and inhaled the musky scent of her arousal and, moving forward to lick into her softness, tasted the wet, honeyed heat of her sex.

Tariq heard her cry out his name, but he was too far gone to reply. He knew only that he had to be inside of her, joined with her. So deep it would not matter what he could or could not say. He stood, his hands rough and desperate on the fly of his trousers. He sighed as he released himself, hard and pulsing with need. Stepping closer, he guided himself with one hand while he gripped her hip with the other, and drove into her depths.

It was perfect. She was perfect.

Tariq pressed his mouth against her neck, her shoulder, as he began to move, driving them both slowly insane with each sure thrust. He felt her stiffen, heard her cry out, and then she shook apart beneath him, moaning again and again. He withdrew, flipping her over even while she continued to gasp through the aftershocks, and settled her on the edge of the bed.

Her face was flushed, her hair in a mad tangle over one shoulder. Still she smiled at him and opened her arms, her eyes reflecting the man she saw in him—the man he wanted to be, and could be, when she looked at him that way.

Tariq moved over her, and slid back inside of her, making them both groan. She braced her hands against his chest. Still clad in his coat and dress shirt, he set a fierce, uncompromising pace. She locked her ankles in the small of his back and arched her breasts toward his mouth. He tasted her flesh, like salt and a sweetness he knew was all Jessa. All his.

When he hurtled over the edge, he took her with him. She shook around him, sobbing out his name like a song.

When he could think again, Tariq stood, pulling her to her feet and helping her out of the gown. Sleepy-eyed and deliciously naked, she crawled back into the bed, and curled on her side to watch him as he pulled off his formal clothes and tossed them in the direction of the nearest chair.

She was his. She belonged to him, whether it made sense or not, whether she knew it or not. She had survived their past and still made love to him with her whole self, body and soul. She had seen him in both of his incarnations, the shameful past as well as the present, and wanted him anyway.

There was more to it than possessiveness, a wide swathe of darker, deeper emotion, but Tariq pushed that aside. The possessiveness he understood. He could not give her up. Not again. He could not lose her unrestrained passion, her unstudied abandon when he touched her. He could not lose *her*. He did not want to think about it any further than that. He did not need to. He knew it to be true with a deep, implacable certainty.

"I must return to Nur," he said abruptly. He saw her tense almost imperceptibly and then drop her eyes to the mattress. "I have been putting it off these past weeks."

"Of course," she murmured, her voice even and yet distant, he thought. The hectic color faded from her cheeks as she stared at her hands. "We must all return to real life eventually. I understand."

How could she understand, when he was not sure he did? But he could easily picture her in the royal palace, wearing silks and jewels that enhanced her quiet beauty, while he made love to her on low pillows or feasted on her lush body in some desert oasis. He could see her against the bright blue skies and the shifting white sands, her eyes mysterious like his people's favorite spices, making him long to taste her over and over again. He saw her in his arms and immediately felt better. Safer, somehow, however illogical that seemed.

"I do not think you do," he said slowly, climbing onto the bed, holding her gaze with his as he prowled toward her on his hands and knees. "I want you to come with me, Jessa. I insist upon it."

"You insist…?" she breathed, but the color returned to her face, red and hot. Her eyes glowed.

He would never let her go again. *Never.*

"I am the king," he said, and pulled her to him once more.

CHAPTER FOURTEEN

"I WILL not hold you to what you said last night," Jessa told him the following morning, not quite meeting his eyes as she sat down at the breakfast table. "About going with you to Nur."

The morning was bright and unseasonably warm for Paris in autumn, which seemed to Jessa like a stark, strange contrast to inside the bedroom suite, where Tariq had taken her once again before she had fully come awake, pushing his way into her morning shower with that intense look in his eyes and driving her to ecstatic screams against the tiles. She was still quivering.

Tariq had called for breakfast to be served on the private balcony outside the bedroom, more secluded than the one she had seen that first night. He wore a dark button-down dress shirt over dark trousers, the coarse silk of his hair brushing the collar. She thought he looked like a warrior god pretending to be at rest, masquerading as some kind of businessman. The early morning sun teased the treetops and casement windows that lined the ancient street in front of her, and made her think she could do what she'd decided she must do in the shattering aftermath of his lovemaking. She pulled her robe tighter around her and touched the wet hair she'd piled atop her head. She could act serene and calm and disinterested over rich black coffee and croissants so soft they seemed like clouds and butter. She could prove that she was no longer that infatuated, broken girl he'd left behind once before.

"Will you not?" He did not glance up from the papers he read, and yet the fine hairs on the back of her neck stood up in warning.

"Of course not," she said, feeling her temper engage and roll through her. Surely he should at least pay attention when she was attempting to be noble! She knew that if she went with him to Nur, she would not be able to maintain even a tenuous grip on the realities of their different situations in life. She knew she would be lost. "I have my own life to be getting back to, in any case."

Tariq laid his papers to the side of his plate and leveled a look at her. Jessa kept herself from squirming in her chair by sheer force of will.

"If you do not wish to accompany me to my country, then say you do not wish it," he said evenly. "But do not wrap it up in some attempt to release me from an obligation. If I did not want you to come, I would not have invited you."

"I was not—" she began, stung, though his words resonated more than she would have liked.

"We leave tomorrow morning," he said, rising to his feet. He crooked his brows as he looked down at her. "You must decide."

"Decide?" she echoed, her heart thumping too hard against her ribs. "Decide what?"

"If you will accompany me of your own free will," he said, his eyes gleaming, "or if I will simply take you."

"You cannot *take* me anywhere!" she gasped, but her

body betrayed her, her sex warming and melting as surely as if he'd touched her with his clever, provocative hands.

"If you say so," he said. He reached down and cupped her cheek with one large hand, his mouth unsmiling and his gaze intent, though still showing his amusement. And still it was as if he was branding her with his touch, his eyes. She felt small, safe and threatened at the same time— and more than that, *his*.

Completely and indisputably his.

His thumb dragged across her full lower lip, sending desire shooting through her body, tightening her nipples, wetting her sex further. Tariq smiled then, as if he could see her body's reaction. One dark eyebrow arched as color heated Jessa's cheeks. Point made, he turned away, disappearing inside the house and leaving her to her ragged breathing and her pounding heart.

He wanted to take her to Nur.

Part of her rejoiced for what that must mean, surely. It meant at the very least that he did not want this idyll in Paris to end any more than she did. But, of course, it was not quite that simple. Jessa drew her legs up beneath her on the chair, and stared out over the city she had come to love over the past dreamlike weeks, as if that could give her the answer.

She could not go to Nur. She could not continue to stay with him, ignoring reality while she played pretend. There were hundreds of reasons she should run back to York as quickly as she could.

And only one reason to stay.

Jessa rested her chin on her drawn-up knees and let out a shuddering breath as the shattering truth washed over her like the Paris sunlight, sweet and bright and unequivocal.

I love him.

She was in love with him. With Tariq, who had hurt her and lied to her. Who she was still lying to, if only by omission. Who she had made love to anyway, deliciously and repeatedly. Whose pain upset her, made her want to comfort and heal him, even when she was what caused it, and even when her own pain matched his. Their complicated, messy history should have made him the last man on earth she could ever have feelings for, but instead she felt closer to him because of it. As if no one could ever really understand her or what she'd been through, more than the man who grieved along with her.

Had she always loved him? Had she never fallen *out* of love with him? He had left and she had been forced to carry on, and she had had reason enough to be furious with him in the abstract, but she had still found her way into his bed within days of laying eyes on him again. She had told herself it was for her own purposes, but the reality was, she hadn't leaped into bed with anyone else. She had never wanted anyone else the way she wanted Tariq.

She wondered if on some level she had deliberately left her bag with her bank card behind when she'd set out for the train—because she hadn't really wanted to leave him.

She wanted to go with him wherever he wanted to take her, even though she knew it was highly likely that he would break her heart when he married someone more appropriate, but she couldn't find it in her to be as worried about that eventuality as she ought to be. It was clear to her now that she had been desperately in love with Tariq since the day she'd first seen him all those years ago, and there was no point in pretending otherwise. Just as there was no point attempting to be noble and leave him first— she might as well enjoy what little time with him she had, the better to hold on to in the lonely years to come.

Because Jessa knew that Tariq could never love her, not after what she had done in giving Jeremy away. How could he, when it was obvious to her that he had wanted his own family so desperately for all of his life? The truth was that she knew, deep down, that she had no right to him. She had been given the opportunity for a second chance, and she was not strong enough to resist it, even though it was clear to her that he would leave her once again.

Jessa uncurled from her chair and stood, staring out at the view but seeing instead his hard, proud face. He didn't have to love her. She would love him enough for them both. She was no stranger to hard love, love like stone, all immovable surfaces and impossibilities. She loved Jeremy more than she had ever thought it possible to love another person, and yet she had given him away, and knew with every breath and every regret that it had been the right decision no matter how much it hurt. She was used to love that bit back and left marks and forced her to be strong.

She could be strong for Tariq, too.

Her sister Sharon was a different story.

"Have you gone mad?" Sharon demanded down the telephone line, sounding scandalized—and uncharacteristically shrill.

Jessa had fortified herself with several cups of the hot, rich coffee from the breakfast service, but it seemed to have done nothing but make her agitated. Or perhaps she was already agitated. She had dressed with extra care, as if Sharon might be able to see her through the telephone and perhaps intuit what Jessa had been doing, but she found that the simple silk blouse and A-line skirt made her feel as insane as Sharon accused her of being. Was she dressing up, pretending to be someone else? Someone more sophisticated that Tariq could love? *Foolish,* she scolded herself, and adjusted her position, holding her mobile close to her ear.

"I don't know how to answer that," she told her sister, which was no more than the truth. She'd settled in for this conversation in the sitting room off the master suite, on the prim settee next to the windows, her back to the breathtaking view of Paris and angled away from the stunning Cézanne painting that took up most of the far wall—she wanted no distractions.

"I thought it was strange enough that you'd run off on a holiday with no advance warning," Sharon continued. "But to get mixed up with that man again? Jessa, how could you?"

"You don't know him," Jessa said evenly, feeling called to protect Tariq, even from her sister who could do him no real harm. Quite the opposite, in fact.

"I know quite enough!" Sharon said with a snort. "I know that he lied to you and left you! I know that men like him think they can swan in and out of people's lives as they please, with no thought to the consequences!"

"Tariq is not the same person he was then," Jessa said. She sighed. "And nothing is really as simple as it might have seemed back then."

"You can do whatever you like with your own life, no matter how reckless, but this isn't just about you, is it?" Sharon let out a ragged breath. "Selfish!" she half whispered, but Jessa heard her perfectly. She could even picture what her sister was doing—pacing the kitchen in her cottage with one arm wrapped around her waist, her face set in a terrible frown—as if she was there to see it in person.

Jessa told herself not to snap back at Sharon. Of course her sister was terrified by the prospect of Jessa with Tariq again. How could she not be? Jessa closed her eyes and lay her palm flat against her chest, just above her heart, as if she could massage away the ache that bloomed there. She could love Sharon, too, because she knew full well that beneath her sister's prickly exterior she loved Jessa in return. Sharon had always been there for Jessa. And wasn't that what love was for, in the end? To embrace others when they most needed it, whether they appreciated it or not?

"I would never do anything to hurt you," Jessa said softly, pinching the top of her nose between her fingers, hoping the headache that had bloomed there would fade. "Any of you. As you should know already. But I am going to go with him." She braced herself. "I have to."

"I can't believe this!" Sharon hissed. "What is it about this man that turns you so dense, Jessa? People don't change. He will hurt you all over again. That's a promise."

Jessa felt as if she'd been in suspended animation for years, with nothing but ice water and regret in her veins, until Tariq had roared back into her life and filled her with heat and life and love. How could she ever regret that, no matter what happened? But she couldn't share that with Sharon.

"I only phoned to let you know that I'll be traveling," Jessa said after a moment, fighting to keep her voice steady, and not to give in to the kick of adrenaline and insecurity that made her want to slap back at her sister. "I'm not asking for your permission."

She opened her eyes again and let them fall on the glorious painting on the wall across from her seat. It was a mountain scene, blues and greens and none of it soothing, somehow, with Sharon so angry.

"I cannot believe that you would risk so much on what? Your *hope* that things might be different?" Sharon made a bitter sort of sound. "I *hope* you haven't gone off the deep end!"

"I hope so, too," Jessa murmured, because there was nothing she could say that could make Sharon feel any better.

Sharon hung up the phone. Jessa let hers drop into her lap, and ordered herself to breathe. Her eyes were wide open this time. She had loved him when nothing about him was true, and she loved him now. Still. Did that make her the fool her sister thought her? Did she mind terribly if it did?

"Who were you talking to?" Tariq asked from the doorway, his low voice making Jessa jump in her seat as if scalded. Her eyes flew to his and she felt the blood drain from her face. She felt raw. Exposed. Had she said anything incriminating? Had she mentioned Jeremy?

"How long have you been standing there?" she asked, trying to sound calm, but her voice was far too high-pitched. Her heart pounded as if she'd just run a mile. It was too much—Sharon's frustrated anger and her own re-alizations about her feelings for Tariq. How could she face him before she had time to pull herself back together?

But it was too late—he was standing right in front of her, and Jessa was suddenly terrified that he could read her like a book.

Guilty. That was the look on her face, he realized after a moment of confusion. Guilty and pale.

"What is the matter?" he asked, searching her expression, all of his senses on red alert. He had finished a meeting more quickly than he'd expected, and had come here hoping to convince her to help him while away the time before the next meeting more pleasurably. He had not expected that he would find her secretive and jumpy. While he watched, she surged to her feet and held her mobile phone behind her, as if hiding it.

"Nothing is the matter," she said, but her voice was too uneven. Tariq felt his instincts kick in, the ones that served him well in politics as well as in combat situations. He moved closer to her.

"Who was that on the phone?" he asked again, this time with less curiosity and more command.

"No one," she said. Then she blinked and smiled, but it was not a real smile. It was far too strained. "It was my sister, Sharon, that's all."

"Did your sister upset you?" he asked. He searched her face. "With your parents gone, you must be close to her and her family."

She flinched, that guilty look stealing across her face again, though this time she tried to hide it. It was an absurd, over-the-top reaction, and he reached out a hand toward her, frowning, worried that something was truly the matter—

And suddenly, somehow, he knew.

The photograph he'd seen in her house flashed before his eyes, the one he'd snatched from the mantel and given only a cursory glance. The sister who looked like Jessa— the same copper-colored hair, the same chin. Her fair-haired, freckled husband.

And their olive-skinned, dark-haired child.

No. He felt himself freeze solid from the inside out, as if he'd been thrown headfirst into a glacier. *She could not have done this and not have told me, not after all of this—*

"Tell me," he said, feeling still, quiet, empty and bleak. "What is the name of your sister's child?"

It was as if he saw her from a great distance then. He saw her face twist into misery. Her hands clenched together in front of her. She was the very picture of distress.

"Tariq," she said, her voice heavy, and he knew it was true. "You don't understand."

All this time he had believed the child lost to him forever, believed that was no more than what he deserved—the reward for his wasted life. And all this time she had smiled so sweetly, made him feel as if she was the family he had longed for—all while knowing exactly where his child, *his son,* was!

"What exactly is it that I do not understand?" he asked her icily, his gaze boring into her. He held himself carefully, afraid that if he moved he would shatter into a rage so hot it would burn him, her, the whole house, the entire damned city. "Were you planning to tell me? Ever?"

"I couldn't," she said, her voice thick, her eyes bright with tears. "It is not my secret to tell."

"That excuse might work, Jessa, were I not the only other person on this earth who has a right to know *at least* as much about the child I never knew I had as you!"

"It is not about you!" she cried, throwing her arms wide. "It's about *him,* Tariq! It's about what *he* needs!"

"You let me think that he was lost to us forever. You *let me* think it!" His whisper was fierce, furious. He could taste the acrid flavor of betrayal in his mouth, feel it corroding him, turning everything he had believed about her—about the two of them—to burned-out husks and charred remains.

"This is exactly the reaction I was trying to prevent!" she cried.

"You have said enough." He silenced her with a slash of his hand through the air, and then he turned and stalked toward the door.

She had never planned to tell him. She had made love to him, comforted him, and had had no intention of telling

him that all the while she knew where his son—his heir—
was. He stopped walking when he reached the doorway,
and stood there for a moment, fighting for control.

"Don't you think I would have noticed the resemblance
at some point?" he asked, not turning back to her. "What
story did you plan to tell me then?"

"When would you have seen him?" she asked after a
moment, sounding genuinely confused. He turned then
and stared at her in disbelief.

"Are you ashamed to be seen with me?" he asked acidly.
"I think it is too late for these protestations, Jessa. You have
been photographed in my company."

"I don't understand what you're talking about!" she
cried. "I didn't think you'd ever lay eyes on him. Why
would you spend time with my family?"

"I told you I was taking you to my country," he snapped
at her. "What do you think that entails?"

"I'm sure you take a thousand women to your country!" she threw back at him, color high in her cheeks, her
eyes dark.

"You are incorrect," he said icily, each word cutting. "I
would never take a woman to my people unless I planned
to keep her. Though that is no longer a subject you need
concern yourself with."

She stared at him in shocked silence. He felt something
move in him, but stamped it down. *No. Damn her.* Her pain
did not, could not, matter—not anymore.

Tariq shook his head and turned back toward the door.

"Please..." she said, though it sounded more like a sob.
"Where are you going?"

The look he threw back at her should have burned her
alive.

"To see my son," he bit out.

And then he strode from the room before he broke something. Before she broke him any further than she already had.

CHAPTER FIFTEEN

OTHER than informing her that her presence was required only to assure him access to the child, Tariq cut her off completely. He did not speak to her on the plane, he merely sat in a thunderous silence that made Jessa ache in ways she would have thought impossible, though she would not let herself dissolve into tears as she wished. He did not speak to her in the car that took them from Leeds to York and then up the York Road toward the North Yorkshire Moors, and the small village along the way where Sharon had moved almost four years ago. Jessa could hardly stand to look at the cultivated fields that spread out on all sides, that intense British green against the cold gray skies. She could see only the coming heartbreak, the doom, the end of everything she had fought so hard to provide for the son she had loved enough to let go. She knew that no one could emerge from it unscathed, not her sister and Barry, not Tariq, not herself.

And worst of all, not Jeremy.

"I don't know what your plan is," Jessa said in a low voice as the car turned into the village and made its way along the high street. It was not the first time she had attempted to speak to him, but there was a desperation in her voice that had not been there before. "You cannot simply arrive at my sister's house and make demands!"

"Watch me," Tariq said, his voice vibrating with the same fury that had gripped him since Paris. He did not look at Jessa. He kept his brooding gaze fixed on the village that slid by outside the window, one elegant hand tapping out his agitation against the armrest.

"Tariq, this is madness!" Jessa cried. "My sister has adopted him! It is all quite legal, and cannot be undone!"

"You will not tell me what can and cannot be undone," he bit out, turning his head to pierce her with his dark, imperious gaze. He was angrier than she'd ever seen him, and all of it so brutally cold, so bitter. "You, who would lie about something like this? Who would conceal a child from his own father? I have no interest in what *you* think I should or should not do!"

"I understand that you're angry," Jessa said, fighting to keep her voice level. He laughed slightly, in disbelief. She set her jaw and forged ahead anyway. "I understand that you think you've been betrayed."

"That I *think* I have been betrayed?" he echoed, his eyes burning into her. He sat as far away from her as it was possible to sit in the enclosed space of the car, and yet she could feel him invading her space, taking her over, crowding her. "I would hate to see what you consider a real betrayal, Jessa, if this does not qualify."

"This is not about you," Jessa said as firmly as she could when she was trembling. "Don't you see? This has nothing to do with me or you. This is about—"

"We are here," he said dismissively, cutting her off as the car pulled up at Sharon's front gate. Tariq did not wait for the driver to get out of the car, he simply threw open his door and climbed out.

Jessa threw herself out after him, her chest heaving as if she'd run a marathon. Tariq paused for a moment outside the gate, and she knew it was now or never. After everything she had sacrificed—including, though it made her want to weep, Tariq himself—she could not let him wreck it all. She had to try one last time.

She lunged forward and grabbed on to his arm, holding him when he might have walked through the gate.

"Release my arm," he said almost tonelessly, though she did not mistake the menace underneath, nor the way he tensed his strong muscles beneath her hands.

"You have to listen to me!" she gasped. "You have to!"

"I have listened to you, and I have listened to you," Tariq said coldly, his eyes black with his anger. "I have watched you weep and I have heard you talk about how much you regret what you had to do, what you did because of me. I did not realize you were still punishing me!"

"It was not because of you!" Jessa cried as the wind cut into her, chilling her. "It was because of me!" She dragged in a wild breath, all the tears she'd been fighting off surging forth, and she simply let them. "I am the one who was so deficient that you left me in the first place, and I am the one who failed so completely as a mother that I couldn't keep my own baby! *Me.*"

She had his attention then. He stilled, his dark eyes intense on hers.

"But I did one thing right," Jessa continued, fighting to keep the tears from her voice. "I made sure he was with people who loved him—who already loved him—who could give him the world. And he is happy here, Tariq, happier than I ever could have made him."

"A child is happiest with his own parents," Tariq said.

Did she imagine that his voice was a trifle less cold? Was it possible?

Jessa stared at him, her fingers flexing into his arm, demanding that he hear her now if he heard her at all.

"He *is* with his parents," she whispered fiercely.

Tariq made a noise that might have been a roar of anger, checked behind the muscle that worked in his jaw. He shook her hands off his arm. Jessa let them drop to her sides.

"He is my blood," he snarled at her. *"Mine!"*

"His family is here," Jessa continued because she had to. Because it was true. "Right here. And he has no idea that he ever had any parents but these."

"Why am I not surprised that your sister would keep this secret as well?" Tariq demanded. "You are a family of liars!"

"He is a little boy who has only ever known *these* parents and *this* home!" Jessa cried. The wind whipped into her, racing down from the moors, and her hair danced between them like a copper flame. She shoved it back. "There's no lie here! They are his parents by law, and in fact. He loves them, Tariq. He *loves* them!"

His hard mouth was set in an obstinate line. "He is not yet five years old. He will learn—"

"You lost your parents, and so did I," Jessa interrupted, her heart pounding so hard in her head, her throat, that she thought she might faint. But she could not, so she did not. She searched his remote, angry face. "You know what it's like to be ripped away from everything you know. *You know!* How could you do that to your own child?"

The door to the cottage opened, and it was as if time stopped.

"Aunt Jessa!" cried the sweet baby voice. Jessa's heart dropped to her shoes.

"Tariq, you cannot do this!" Jessa hissed at him

urgently, but she did not think he heard her. He had gone pale, and still. Slowly, he turned.

And everything ended, then and there.

My son.

Tariq stared at the boy, unable to process what he was seeing. It had been one thing to rage about a child in the abstract, and quite another to see a small, mischievous-looking little boy, still chubby of cheek and wild of hair from an earlier sleep, toddle out the front door.

Tariq was frozen into place, unable to move, as the boy scampered down the steps. Jessa threw a look over her shoulder as she moved to intercept the child, scooping him up into her arms. She murmured something Tariq couldn't hear, which made the boy laugh and wiggle in her grasp.

The boy. Why could he not bring himself to use the child's name? *Jeremy.*

Another figure appeared at the door. Jessa's sister. She looked at the scene in front of her and blanched, telling Tariq that she knew exactly who he was. For a moment she and Tariq locked eyes, both struck still.

"Jessa," the other woman said, keeping her voice calm for the child's benefit though her eyes remained on Tariq, wary and scared. "What are you doing here? I thought you were on holiday."

Jessa shifted and put the little boy back on the ground. "I was," she said. She shrugged, half apology and half helplessness. "We thought we would stop by."

She looked at Tariq then, her cinnamon eyes swimming with tears. She put out her hand and cupped the top of Jeremy's head in her palm.

Jeremy, Tariq thought. *My son's name is Jeremy.*

"How lovely," the sister said, her voice strained. "You know how much Jeremy loves his aunt."

Jessa stood before him, still touching the little boy, her gaze silently imploring. Tariq felt something rip apart inside of him, and the pain was so intense for a moment that he could not tell if what he felt was emotional or physical.

Jeremy shook off Jessa's hand, his dark eyes fixed on the stranger he only just then seemed to notice standing before him. Tariq's heart stopped in his chest as the little boy moved toward him in his lurching, jerky dance of a walk, stopping when he could peer up from beneath his thick black hair. He was close enough to touch, and yet Tariq could not move.

His eyes were the same dark green as Tariq's. Tariq felt the impact of them like a body blow, but he did not react, he only returned the solemn, wide-eyed stare that was directed at him. Jeremy was as much Jessa's child as his. Tariq could see her in the boy's fairer skin, the shape of his eyes and brows, and that defiant little chin.

"Hello, Jeremy," Tariq said, his voice thick. "I am…"

He paused, and he could feel the tension emanating from both Jessa and her sister. He could almost hear it. He glanced over and saw that Jessa's sister had covered her mouth with her hands, her eyes wide and fearful. And then there was Jessa, who watched him with her heart in her gaze and tears making slow tracks down her cheeks. She stood with her arms at her sides, defeated, waiting for him to destroy everything she had worked so hard to protect.

She mouthed the word, *Please*.

"I am Tariq," he said at last, gazing back down into eyes so like his own, because it was the only thing he could think of that was not threatening to anyone, and was also true.

Jeremy blinked.

Then he let out a giggle and turned back around, to hurtle himself toward the door of the cottage and toward the woman who stood there, still holding her hands over her mouth as if holding back a scream. He buried his face against her leg, his small arms grabbing on to her in a spontaneous hug. Then he tilted back his face, lit from within with the purest, most uncomplicated love that Tariq had ever seen.

"Hi Mommy," Jeremy chirped, oblivious to the drama being played out around him.

Jessa's sister smiled down at him, then looked back at Tariq, her own face stamped with the same love, though hers was fiercer, more protective. But no less pure.

Tariq felt his heart break into a thousand pieces inside his chest, and scatter like dust.

Tariq stood by the gate, his back to the cottage, while Jessa carried on a rushed conversation with her sister. She kept sneaking looks at his strong, proud back, wondering what he must be feeling rather than paying attention to Sharon. When her sister finally went inside and closed the door, she hurried down the path to his side.

He did not look at her. He kept his eyes trained on the fields across the lane, that swept to the horizon.

"Thank you," she said, with all the feeling she'd tried to hide from Jeremy. And even from Sharon.

"I did not do anything that requires thanks," Tariq said stiffly. Bitterly.

"You did not ruin a little boy's life, when you could have and have been well within your rights," Jessa said quietly. "I'll thank you for that for the rest of my life."

"I have no rights, as you have been at great pains to advise me."

"I am sorry," she said. She stepped closer to him, forcing him to look at her. His eyes seemed so sad that it made her want to weep. Without thinking, she reached out and grabbed hold of his hand. "I am so sorry."

"So am I," he said quietly, almost letting the wind snatch it away. He looked down at their joined hands. "More than I can say."

She would not cry for him, not now, not when he held himself so aloof. She knew what that must mean—it was inevitable, really, after what they'd just been through. Jessa took a deep breath and forced herself to smile as she let go of him. She wanted to hold him and kiss him until the remoteness left him and he was once again alive and wild in her arms. She wanted to share the pain of leaving Jeremy behind, and make it easier, somehow, for both of them to bear. Oh, the things she wanted!

But she had always known that she could not have this man. Not for good. And she knew that he had lost something of far greater significance today than her. She could let him go just as she had let Jeremy go. It was the only way she knew how to love them both.

"You should return to Nur as you planned," she said, proud that her voice was even, and showed none of her inner turmoil. She could let him go. She could. "Your country needs you."

So do I! something inside of her screamed, but she bit it back, forced it down. He had never been hers to keep. She had known that from the start.

He seemed to look at her from very far away. He blinked, and some of the darkness receded, letting the green back in. Jessa felt a hard knot ease slightly inside her chest.

"And what about you?" he asked, something she couldn't read passing across his face.

Jessa shrugged, shoving her hands into her pockets so that the fists she'd made could not betray her. "I'll return to York, of course," she said.

The wind surged between them, cold and fierce. Jessa met his gaze and hoped hers was calm. She could do this. And if she broke down later, when she was alone, who would have to know?

"Is this your revenge, then?" he asked, his voice soft though there was a hardness around his eyes. "You wait until I am bleeding and then you turn the knife? Is this what I deserve for what you think I did to you five years ago?"

"No!" she gasped, as stunned as if he'd hit her. Her head reeled. "We are both to blame for what happened five years ago!"

"I am the one who left," Tariq said bitterly.

"You had no choice," Jessa replied. "And I was the one so silly she ran away for days. I left first." She shook her head. "And how can we regret it? We made a beautiful child, a perfect child."

"He is happy here." Tariq said it as if it were fact, a statement, but Jessa could see the pain and uncertainty in the dark sheen of his gaze.

"He is," she whispered fiercely. "I promise you, he is."

She didn't know what to do with the ache inside of her, the agony of feeling so apart from him. She was not the desperate, deeply depressed girl she had been when she had given Jeremy up. She was stronger now, and she knew that the way she loved Tariq was not like the infatuation of her youth. It was tempered with the suffering she'd endured, the way she had come to know him now, as the man she had always imagined him to be.

It might be that she could not bear to make this sacrifice after all.

He is not for you, she told herself fiercely. *Don't make this harder than it already is!*

"Come," Tariq said. He nodded toward the car. "I cannot be here any longer."

Jessa looked back at the cottage, so cozy and inviting against the bleakness of the autumn fields, and yet a place she would always associate with this particular mourning—the kind she imagined might fade and change but would never entirely disappear. She pulled her coat tighter around her. Then she put her arm through Tariq's and let him walk her to the car.

Jessa sat beside him in the plush backseat, feeling his grief as keenly as her own, as sharp as the wind still ripping down from the moors. Tariq did not speak for some time, his attention focused out the window, watching as fields gave way to villages, and villages to towns, as they made their way back through the country toward the city of York. Next to him, Jessa knew that his mind and his heart were still back at her sister's cottage, held tight in Jeremy's sticky little hands. She knew because hers were and, to some extent, always would be.

She had to hope that it would grow easier, as, indeed, in many ways it already had in the past few years. Seeing Jeremy thrive—seeing him happy and so deeply loved—healed parts of herself she had not known were broken. She hoped that someday it would do the same for Tariq.

"I do not know what family means," Tariq said in a low voice. He turned toward her, catching her by surprise, seeming to fill the space between them. "I have never had anyone look at me the way that boy looked at your sister. His mother." His gaze was so fierce then that it made Jessa catch her breath. "Except you. Even now, after everything I have done to you."

Their eyes locked. He reached over and tucked a stray curl behind her ear, then took her face in his hands. The warmth of his touch sped through her veins, heating her from within.

"I have already lost a son," he said, his voice almost too low, as if it hurt him. "I cannot lose you, Jessa. Not you, too."

Joy eased into her then, nudging aside the grief. It was a trickle at first, and then, as he continued to look at her with his face so open, so honest, it widened until it flowed—a hard and complex kind of joy, flavored with all they had lost and all the ways they were tied together.

She reached across the space between them, over her fears and their shared grief, and slid her hand up to hold him as he held her—holding that strong, harsh face, looking deep into the promises in his dark green eyes.

"Then you won't," she whispered as if it were a vow.

She would let the fear go this time, instead of him.

She would love him as long as he let her.

CHAPTER SIXTEEN

HE HEARD her laughter before he saw her.

Tariq strode down the wide palace corridor, past the ancient tapestries and archaeological pieces that told the story of Nur's long history in each successive niche along the way. The floor beneath his feet was tiled, mosaics stretching before him and behind him, all in vibrant colors as befit the royal palace of a king. When he reached the wide, arched doors that opened into the palace's interior courtyard, he paused.

Jessa was so beautiful, she took his breath away. She was a shock of cinnamon and copper against the brilliant blue sky, the white walls, and the palm trees that clanked gently overhead in the afternoon breeze. She seemed brighter to him than the vivid flowering plants that spilled from the balconies on the higher floors, and the sparkle of the fountain in the courtyard's center. She had set aside her novel and was watching the antics of two plump little birds who danced on the fountain's edge. She wore a long linen tunic over loose trousers in the fashion of his people, her feet in thonged sandals. Around her neck she wore a piece of jade suspended from a chain that she had found in one of the city's marketplaces.

She looked as if she belonged exactly where she was.

Mine, he thought, not for the first time.

He crossed to her, smiling when she seemed to sense him and glanced around—smiling more when her face lit up.

"I thought you would be gone until tomorrow," she said, her delight evident in her voice, in the gleam in her eyes, though she did not throw herself into his arms as she might have in a less public area of the palace.

"My business concluded early," he said. He had made sure of it—he wanted to be away from Jessa less and less. In some sense, she was the only family he had ever known. What they had lost together made him feel more bound to her than he had ever been to another human being. And he could think of only one way to ensure that he never need be apart from her again. The birds chattered at him from their new perch on the higher rim of the fountain. "You have been here nearly a month and still you are fascinated by the birds?" He eyed her. "Perhaps you should get out more."

"Perhaps I should," she agreed. He watched as her gaze shuttered, hiding her feelings from him as she still did from time to time whenever any hint of a discussion of their future appeared. It was time to end it.

"As a matter of fact," he said quietly, "that is what I wanted to talk to you about."

"Getting out?" she asked, frowning slightly.

"In a manner of speaking," he said. He looked down at her, wanting to pull her into his arms and kiss his way into this discussion. That seemed to be the language in which they were both fluent. "I want to talk about the future. You and me."

Jessa went very still. The splash of water in the fountain behind her was all Tariq heard for a long moment, while her eyes went dark.

Then she lifted her chin, defiant and brave to the end. "There is no need," she said with a certain grace, drawing herself up and onto her feet. She picked up her book and tucked it underneath her arm with stiff, jerky movements. "I have always known this day was coming."

"Have you?" he asked mildly.

"Of course," she said briskly. "One of the first things you told me when you walked into my office was that you needed to get married. Naturally, you must do your duty to your country."

She held her head high as she skirted around him. She headed across the courtyard and up the wide steps toward his private quarters. Tariq followed, watching the sway of her hips in the soft linen and admiring the ramrod straightness of her spine. He followed her inside the palace and all the way into the vast bedroom suite, where he leaned against the bed and watched her look wildly around, as if searching for something.

"Never fear," she said in the same false tone, turning to face him. "I have no intention of making this awkward for either of us. I will simply pack a few things and be out of your way in no time."

She looked as if she might change her mind and bolt for the door.

"You are so determined to leave me," he drawled, amused. "It is almost a shame that I have no intention of letting you do so."

She froze in place, her face expressionless while her eyes burned hot.

"What do you mean?" she asked, her voice little more than a whisper.

"What do you think I mean?" he asked.

For a moment she only stared at him.

"I will not be in your *harem!*" she muttered, scandalized. "How could you suggest such a thing?"

"I am not planning to collect a harem." His mouth crooked up in one corner. "Assuming, of course, you behave."

"I don't understand," she whispered, though it was more like a sob.

"You do." He moved closer to her, so he could reach out and hold her by her slender shoulders. "You have simply decided it cannot happen. I do not know why."

Her mouth worked, and she flushed a deep, hot red.

"You must have a queen who is worthy of you," she said after a moment. "One who is your equal in every way."

"I must have *you*," he replied simply, leaning forward to kiss her. Her lips clung to his for a long, sweet moment, and then she pulled back to frown at him.

"No," she said firmly.

"No?"

"I won't marry you," she gritted out, and moved out of his grip. She rubbed at her arms for a moment, her head bent.

Tariq ordered himself to be patient. "Why not?" he asked, in a far easier tone than the possessiveness that clawed at him demanded.

She looked at him. Her lips pressed together, and her hands balled into fists at her side.

"I love you," she blurted out, and then sighed slightly, as if it hurt to say aloud, even as sweet triumph washed through Tariq—making him want to roar out his victory, shout it from the rooftops. When she looked at him again, her eyes were overly bright, but her chin was high. "I cannot marry a man who does not love me," she said. Bravely and definitively. "Not even you."

Tariq closed the distance between them, his expression unreadable. But this was not about sex, explosive as it had always been between them. This was about something bigger.

That must be why she wanted to collapse into sobs.

"Don't!" Jessa whispered, though she did not move—did not make any attempt to avoid him. "This is hard enough, Tariq! Please do not—"

He silenced her with his mouth upon hers, his hand fisting in the mess of her curls. He kissed her until she melted against him, soft and pliant against his hardness despite everything, until her arms crept around his neck and she kissed him back with a matching ferocity. He kissed her until she couldn't tell who moaned, who sighed, while the fire of their connection raged between them, incinerating them both in a delicious blaze.

"I love you," he told her in a low voice when he tore his mouth away from hers, his gaze dark and green and so serious it made Jessa gasp.

She searched his face, not daring to believe she had heard him right. She even shook her head, as if to refute it.

Tariq smiled.

"I have never loved another woman," he said. "I never will. How can you doubt it? I longed for you for five long years. I hunted you to the ends of the earth."

"York is not the ends of the earth," she said, absurdly. He traced a line down her jaw, still smiling.

"That depends where you start." He sighed. "Jessa. What are you so afraid of? Did I not tell you what would happen if I brought you here?"

She remembered he had been angry, but she also remembered what he had said—that he would keep any woman he brought to his palace. But she could not seem to get her head around it. She could not seem to believe.

"That was a long time ago," Jessa whispered.

"I will marry you," he said, as if there had never been any other possibility.

"You cannot!" she cried, hard emotions racking her, fear scraping through her, leaving her trembling in his arms. "I do not deserve you! Not after—" Her eyes swam with tears, blurring the world, but she could still see him, so strong and intent. "I gave him away, Tariq. I gave him up."

"And we will miss him," Tariq replied after a moment, his voice thick with his own emotions. "Together."

Jessa let out a breath and, with it, something tight and frozen seemed to thaw, letting light and hope begin to trickle through her. Letting her wonder, *what if?*

He pressed his lips against her forehead. In a softer tone, yet no less demanding, no less sure, he said, "And we will have another child, Jessa. Not as a replacement. Never as a replacement. As a new beginning. This I promise you."

The tears spilled over now, wetting her cheeks. She touched his face, an echo of that cold day when Tariq had finally understood the magnitude of what she had given up, and why. Jeremy would be an ache they carried with them for the rest of their lives, day in and day out. But for the first time, she dared to hope that they would carry it together across the years, making it easier to bear that way. And someday, only if he wished it, they would tell Jeremy the story of how much he was loved, and how well.

"Yes," she breathed, her heart too full to let her smile. "We will be a family."

"We will," he said gruffly, and something powerful and true swelled between them then, and seemed to spread out around them to fill the room.

The thought of making a child with Tariq—deliberately—in joy and in love, and then raising that child together as she had always wanted to believe they were meant to do… It was almost too overwhelming.

Almost.

"I haven't agreed to any marriage," Jessa told Tariq then, with a small smile, while an intoxicating cocktail of hope and joy surged through her. She could feel it inexorably changing her with every second. Could dreams come true after all, after everything they had been through? After all that they had done? Was it possible?

Looking at him, she dared to believe it for the first time.

She was still twined around him, her legs astride one of his and her sex pressed intimately against his thigh. He moved slightly and made her groan as that sweet, delirious heat rocked through her.

"I suggest you get used to the idea," Tariq said, a smile in his voice, his eyes. "This is my country. I do not require your agreement." He kissed her again, capturing her lower lip between his teeth for a moment before releasing her. He smiled. "Though I would like it."

"Yes," she said softly, wonder rolling through her, making her feel as incandescent as the desert sun. Only with Tariq. Only for him. "Yes, I will marry you."

"You will be happy, Jessa," he vowed, fiercely, sweeping her up off the floor, high against his chest. She wrapped her legs around his waist and gripped tight to his shoulders, looking down at him as he held her. At the jade eyes that so consumed her that she had bought a necklace to match, so she might have something like him to look at when he was away. At this man she had loved for so long, and in so many different ways. Her playboy lover. Her king. *Her husband.*

"You will be happy," he said again, frowning at her as if he dared her to disagree.

"Is that your royal decree?" she asked, laughing as he whirled her around and tipped her backward onto the soft bed behind them. He fell with her, following her down and then bracing himself on his arms before he crashed into her.

"I am the king," he said, leaning over her. "My word is law."

"I am to be the queen," she said, shivering slightly as the idea of it began to truly take hold. She would have this man forever. She would be able to hold him like this, love him like this. She felt her eyes well up as she reached between them to trace his mouth, the hard planes of his face. Harsh, forbidding. *Hers*.

"So my word should also be law, should it not?" she asked.

"If you wish it."

Jessa smiled and lifted her head to kiss him, sweet and more sure than she had ever been of anything.

"Then *we* will be happy," she said and, for the first time, truly believed it, with all of her heart and soul. "Because I say so."

LARGER-PRINT BOOKS!

HARLEQUIN *Presents*~

PASSION GUARANTEED SEDUCTION

GET 2 FREE LARGER-PRINT NOVELS PLUS 2 FREE GIFTS!

YES! Please send me 2 FREE LARGER-PRINT Harlequin Presents® novels and my 2 FREE gifts (gifts are worth about $10). After receiving them, if I don't wish to receive any more books, I can return the shipping statement marked "cancel". If I don't cancel, I will receive 6 brand-new novels every month and be billed just $4.55 per book in the U.S. or $5.24 per book in Canada. That's a saving of at least 13% off the cover price! It's quite a bargain! Shipping and handling is just 50¢ per book.* I understand that accepting the 2 free books and gifts places me under no obligation to buy anything. I can always return a shipment and cancel at any time. Even if I never buy another book, the two free books and gifts are mine to keep forever.

176/376 HDN E5NG

Name	(PLEASE PRINT)	
Address		Apt. #
City	State/Prov.	Zip/Postal Code

Signature (if under 18, a parent or guardian must sign)

Mail to the **Harlequin Reader Service:**
IN U.S.A.: P.O. Box 1867, Buffalo, NY 14240-1867
IN CANADA: P.O. Box 609, Fort Erie, Ontario L2A 5X3

Not valid for current subscribers to Harlequin Presents Larger-Print books.

Are you a subscriber to Harlequin Presents books and want to receive the larger-print edition? Call 1-800-873-8635 today!

* Terms and prices subject to change without notice. Prices do not include applicable taxes. Sales tax applicable in N.Y. Canadian residents will be charged applicable provincial taxes and GST. Offer not valid in Quebec. This offer is limited to one order per household. All orders subject to approval. Credit or debit balances in a customer's account(s) may be offset by any other outstanding balance owed by or to the customer. Please allow 4 to 6 weeks for delivery. Offer available while quantities last.

Your Privacy: Harlequin Books is committed to protecting your privacy. Our Privacy Policy is available online at www.eHarlequin.com or upon request from the Reader Service. From time to time we make our lists of customers available to reputable third parties who may have a product or service of interest to you. If you would prefer we not share your name and address, please check here. ☐

Help us get it right—We strive for accurate, respectful and relevant communications. To clarify or modify your communication preferences, visit us at www.ReaderService.com/consumerchoice.

HPLP10R

HARLEQUIN®

A Romance

FOR EVERY MOOD™

Spotlight on

Inspirational

Wholesome romances
that touch the heart and soul.

See the next page
to enjoy a sneak peek from
the Love Inspired® Suspense
inspirational series.

*See below for a sneak peek from
our inspirational line, Love Inspired® Suspense*

*Enjoy this heart-stopping excerpt from
RUNNING BLIND
by top author Shirlee McCoy,
available November 2010!*

**The mission trip to Mexico was supposed to be an
adventure. But the thrill turns sour when Jenna Dougherty
and her roommate Magdalena are kidnapped.**

"It's okay. I'm here to help." The voice was as deep as the
darkness, but Jenna Dougherty didn't believe the lie. She
could do nothing but lie still as hands slid down her arms,
felt the rope around her wrists.

"I'm going to use a knife to cut you free, Jenna. Hold
still."

The cold blade of a knife pressed close to her head before
her gag fell away.

"I—" she started, but her mouth was dry, and she could
do nothing but suck in air.

"Shhh. Whatever needs to be said can be said when
we're out of here." Nick spoke quietly, his hand gentle on
her cheek. There and gone as he sliced through the ropes on
her wrists and ankles.

He pulled her upright. "Come on. We may be on
borrowed time."

"I can't leave my friend," Jenna rasped out.

"There's no one here. Just us."

"She has to be here." Jenna took a step away.

"There's no one here. Let's go before that changes."

"It's dark. Maybe if we find a light…"

"What did you say?"

SHLISEXP1110

"We need to turn on the light. I can't leave until I know that—"

"What can you see, Jenna?"

"Nothing."

"No shadows? No light?"

"No."

"It's broad daylight. There's light spilling in from the window I climbed in through. You can't see it?"

She went cold at his words.

"I can't see anything."

"You've got a nasty bruise on your forehead. Maybe that has something to do with it." His fingers traced the tender flesh on her forehead.

"It doesn't matter *how* it happened. I'm blind!"

Can Nick help Jenna find her friend or will chasing this trail have Jenna running blindly again into danger?

Find out in RUNNING BLIND, available in November 2010 only from Love Inspired Suspense.

SHLISEXP1110